A Vine to Prune

BOOK 2 OF THE SPIRIT WIND SERIES

DANIEL DYDEK

BEORN

BEORN PUBLISHING, LLC

Dedication

For Mom and Dad, who modeled love for me;
and for Erin, who loves me

Contents

Chapter 1

The storm clouds massed for days, and I began to wonder if they were my imagination only—or some vision from Our Father. But by the fourth day Mahmoud had noticed and grew nervous. Thomas too, one night, confessed to me he had known strange things might happen around me but expected them to happen a little more suddenly. I could only smile weakly and shrug.

The presence within me had dwindled to barely a mustard seed. By week's end I found myself wishing my hand would catch fire again, and had to laugh. How many days and nights had I spent with the Sisters wishing the Sacred Fire would go away? At least until Bruce's undead army arrived and that fire was the only thing that could dead them again.

Now I spent nights in contemplation and prayer, and would find the seed burning brightly. But, like Thomas, I often wished that whatever was going to happen next would happen. But each village or hamlet we passed through seemed plain enough, and the seed lay dormant.

We needn't have rushed.

By midweek, the second after leaving the convent, the storm clouds were nearly overhead. We came over a sharp fold of ground that dropped below us into a broad plain. In the midst of that plain, centered on a crossroad that ran east toward the mountains, was the largest village we had come to so far. Not quite big enough to be called a town, but sprawling and with a few larger homes and what appeared to be a villa. Fields lay mostly fallow this late in autumn, nearly winter, though some stretches of barley were past midway to harvest.

As we neared, spots of color showed within the village. Streamers of bright colors bedecked many a house, and some were stretched across the road where the buildings allowed. A flower-strewn sign on the road announced it as the village of Aurden. I felt the seed begin to stir.

The road we were on became cobblestone, as was the crossroad. The alleys and pathways between the houses and shops, though, were only packed earth. The streets were not full, but there was more traffic than we had yet encountered. Most smiled at us, nodding graciously or calling out a blessed or beautiful day. Children chased after a hoop, a pair of dogs baying behind them. Near the center of the village was a mule train, and even the dozen guards seemed happy despite their task. Mahmoud, too, was suddenly in good spirits.

"Have you been through here before?" I asked. He seemed to know where he was going.

But after a moment he shook his head. "Your Mother brought me from further east."

We came to the inn, perched on the north-east corner of the cross, two stories tall but with additional windows peeping out of eaves and bulbous folds in the roof. Mahmoud went inside to inquire about rooms while Thomas and I stayed with the mule. A group of men went boisterously down the street as we waited—drunk, it seemed, but happy.

Thomas glanced at me, a question hinting in his eyes. He had done much the same in each village. But now I looked at the streamers and smiles and laughter and ease, and then up at the storm clouds almost black, and the seed sprouted a flame that burned small but intense.

"It seems a little...strange, to me," I said.

"What do you feel?"

I shook my head. "Nothing specific yet, but the Fire in me is wakening. And why is everyone so...pleasant?" I looked at him sheepishly, and he returned a lopsided grin. "I know; why shouldn't people be happy? And why is pleasantness strange? But it is, isn't it?"

He gave a begrudging nod. "There's a lot more than there was in any other village. And with those clouds overhead..." He trailed off as he glanced up, and shuddered. "I just wish it would rain already and be done."

I had to agree. "But, maybe only once we're inside," I said, and we both grinned. The pleasantness seemed to be contagious.

Mahmoud came out. "They are short on rooms," he said. "We will need to occupy only one, and it is not large."

I glanced at him quizzically, then at Thomas with some consternation. "That is not...seemly," I said warily.

Mahmoud shook his head. "Another will open by tonight," he said. "That one will be yours." He took the mule by the halter and led it toward the stables in back. We helped unload as the skies grew impossibly darker. When we came out and made for the inn's entrance it seemed nearly night. The streets were emptying slowly, almost unwillingly. The breeze was quickening and the streamers flapped noisily, their bright colors stark. In the middle of the approaching storm they still sent a ray of joy.

As Mahmoud opened the door the first fat drop struck the cobblestones with a clap, and I startled. We spared one glance for the sky before ducking hurriedly inside. As the door shut behind us the rains came like the drumming of a thousand drummers.

Every patron in the common room looked over, smiles quickly covering their surprise. "Brought the rains with ye, did ye?" someone called, and there was scattered laughter as they returned to their food and drink.

But the rain even from inside roared, and beams creaked as the wind struck the inn. Thomas looked even more troubled than I. But before I could ask, Mahmoud was guiding us through to the stairway in the back. We went up two flights. They had given me the smallest portion of the load, but I still puffed and struggled. Walking miles will only harden someone so far; stairs are an entirely different matter. But I still wished I was more capable, especially when Thomas glanced back at me with a bemused grin. I ducked my head toward my load, cheeks flushed.

Mahmoud finally led us to the room down a narrow hallway. By the sound of the rain, and the peak in the hallway, we must have been directly under the roof. The room was, as he said, "not large"; most of it was made by the protrusion of the window out over the street. The wind, thankfully, was behind us else I fear the rain would have smote through the thin-paned window. Outside looked almost white, and I could not see the street at all.

We set the things down in what corners we could find. There was one bed, a chair, and a small table. Above the table on the wall was a lantern, unlit, and a bundle of rushes for lighting on a shelf beside it. I glanced around, then at Thomas and Mahmoud. It had been cold when we first entered, but I felt our body heat was already warming the small space.

"Where will you sleep?" I asked neither of them in particular, noting the narrow bed that even I would barely fit on.

"I will sleep on the floor," Mahmoud said quickly. I glanced at Thomas to see if he heard the same strange tone in Mahmoud's voice, a slight resignation it sounded like to me. But a resignation he was familiar with.

"We can switch nights," Thomas offered.

Mahmoud's dark eyes glittered. "We will not be here that long," he said.

Thomas glanced warily at me, and I looked at Mahmoud. "I think we—or I—will be," I said slowly.

Mahmoud considered me a moment. "This is no great town," he said.

I smiled. "Neither was Holden, or the convent for that matter."

Mahmoud placed a hand quickly on his side where he had been stabbed, and a quick pain flashed across his eyes. "Well enough," he said. "I have business to the east. Perhaps I will come back for you," he said.

"Mahmoud," Thomas began, but I smiled.

"That's fine," I said quickly. "You were never bound to us as we are never bound to you—at least, by no oath of mine." I looked at Thomas, who finally shrugged.

"Where will you stay?" Mahmoud asked slowly.

I looked around the room. "Here?" I said tentatively. But Mahmoud was already shaking his head.

"We were most fortunate to come today," he said. "The innkeeper assured me there would be no rooms after tonight."

"Why?" Thomas and I chorused.

"There is to be a wedding, of their mayor, to a..." he gesticulated.

"An important lady. I forget the word. The fluttering colors," he added, gesturing to the window where the rain still came down in sheets. The ribbons were for the wedding.

"And why everyone is so happy," Thomas said.

The fire in me flickered. That explanation still did not sit well with me. There was something tenuous about the attitudes I saw, but I couldn't explain so I simply nodded. Of course marriages were wonderful, happy affairs—generally—but for it to infect an entire village, even travelers, that seemed like a greater power to me. And, of course, the Fire seemed to agree.

We went down to dinner. Mahmoud—perhaps because it was his last night with us for a time—was most generous and we enjoyed roast beef in gravy, lentil soup, and slabs of warm brown bread. I sensed, too, it would be the last meal like this for a long time. Thomas and I had little coin left. Even when I said we would stay in the inn, I knew we had no way to pay for it. The lack of rooms only spared us the embarrassment of saying so.

I glanced around the room as we ate, observing the other patrons. A young man with a bittern played in the corner, though his notes only occasionally rose above the pounding rain and the murmuring. Here there still remained some of the joy we had seen on our way in, perhaps a little damped. We had certainly seen more boisterous rooms on our way south. But those had seemed fueled primarily by beer and wine. Here those drinks flowed a little slower, and the revelry was more like a deep lake than a tossing sea. Yet even in that depth there was an impermanence. Not that it was forced—I had considered perhaps they had been ordered to be joyful for the sake of their mayor, or the lady. If she had a title, I wondered if she was conceited. But there is a strain in forced happiness that always breaks through here and there. This felt more like an unfamiliarity, that the slightest thing might return them all suddenly to—if not despair—at least a hardworking grimness. But, those were all guesses.

As we were finishing, the innkeeper informed us my room was ready. We thanked him, Mahmoud left coin, and we went back up through the narrow stairways and halls. We came to Mahmoud's room and he turned aside.

"I want to talk to Rae-Anna for a moment," Thomas said. "Figure out what we're going to do next."

I sensed he was not telling all. But I opened the door, left it open as Thomas went and stood near the window. My room was nearly identical to Mahmoud's, except in here were the remains of some writing implements. I wondered briefly who had stayed here.

"What are we going to do next?" he asked without preamble.

I went to the bed and sat down. "I'm not sure," I said. "We'll need to find somewhere to stay, I guess. We're not without our means—" I cut off as he sighed and stared out the window. "Thomas, what is it?"

"I don't have this Fire you have," he said slowly. "I mean, I do, I guess, but I don't know how to use it. But..." He looked at me. "I understand there's something wrong here. I know what I said to Mahmoud, but I didn't think he would understand. He's not...I mean, he's a Moor."

"Still loved by Our Father, though," I said.

"Is he?" Thomas asked sharply. He turned away again. "I'm sorry, I guess you would know. But here is what I know: that rain out there is destroying the winter crops and turning roads into bogs. There will be nothing to farm, and reduced trade. And in Holden, much less than that turned the people sullen and quiet. And no wedding, no matter how important, would bring them out of it—the families of the bride and groom, perhaps. But not the entire village."

"And that's why we must stay, I think," I said. "There is something else at work here—it might not be as powerful or as evil as Bruce, but if Our Father called us here it was not to destroy us."

Thomas turned to me again as he drew a deep breath, a tentative smile barely reaching his eyes. "Hopefully not yet," he said. A pale joke. But as we gazed at each other, I felt something else stirring in me, a different fire altogether that I felt in my cheeks. His smile strengthened, but then pain too flashed across his eyes and he looked away again.

The fire sucked out of me with an icy blast made worse for the remembered warmth. "Thomas?" I said, hating that my voice quavered at the end.

"I'm sorry, Rae-Anna," he said faintly. "I'm afraid some wounds aren't healed so quickly as Mahmoud's."

I felt my eyes sting, though no tears came yet. I reached out and laid a hand on his arm. He yanked it back in reflex. I almost wish he had taken my arm out of its socket with him—the pain could not have been worse, I thought. Then he turned abruptly and left the room, and I realized I was wrong. I stared at the gaping door for a long time, then managed to get up and shut it. I fell into my bed and wept—for him, I thought. But I knew bitterly that I wept for myself.

A sharp crash of thunder woke me. I was sprawled face down on the bed, still fully clothed and booted, and the pillow was damp. The room was pitch-black, the window a square of indigo on the wall. I realized the rain had lessened. And I heard a tapping of wood on stone.

I scrubbed a hand down my face and stood, stretching muscles stiff from the awkward way in which I had laid. The tapping grated. Slow, rhythmic, and obnoxiously loud. And yet, it came from outside.

I frowned. Why would someone be hammering with all their

might at this hour? I went to the window, realizing for the first time that it overlooked the street. The eaves dripped like a waterfall, but the rain itself was a drizzle. Between drips and runnels on the window I could see the road dimly, and the knock continued to grow louder.

Lightning flashed, and I saw five figures in cowled robes walking down the street, arrayed in a V-shape. The one in the lead carried a staff, from which seemed to come the knocking. I blinked and shook my head; the knocking seemed more in my head than coming from that staff—how could it? He strode normally—perhaps a little slowly, especially given the rain—but it was not as though he banged it like a gavel. And surely others would be throwing open windows to complain of the noise if he were.

Unless they came for me alone.

I opened my own window, to try to see better if nothing else. The banging continued. I could see a little better now, saw a medallion on the tip of his staff. They continued slowly, then stopped in front of the inn. The tapping continued. I found I was holding my breath.

Somewhere a break opened in the clouds, and the moon shone through, striking the five figures. Another flash of lightning, and they looked swiftly up at me. Whether it was a trick of the moon, I don't know. But their faces were ghostly pale, almost maggot-white, their eyes dark sockets. But not like the skeletons in the convent, these had sparkling chips like frost in their depths.

Lightning flashed again, close. When I blinked, the figures were gone from down below. I glanced up and down the street. The rain lessened further, and I realized the tapping had ceased.

I heard a hiss like steam, and I whirled. The men were in my room, staring at me with teeth bared. The leader's head snapped sideways, his rictus curving slowly into a smile. He tipped his staff toward me. I saw the medallion now carved with strange spirals in a vague star-pattern.

Instinctively my left hand came up. The blue flame did not come to it, yet I felt the Fire inside me rage forward. But the men did not recoil, or disappear, or make any comforting move other than withdrawing the staff.

Fasssinating... It came as though the leader whispered into my mind. He licked his teeth with an ash-gray tongue. As the other four took a half-step backward, he stepped forward—as though I were his to claim.

For a moment I quailed and my hand dropped to my side, but the Fire raged higher. "I already belong to another, against whom you have no power," I said quietly, firmly.

"Do you, indeed?" he sneered. "I think he pulled away from you and left swiftly. I think he is disssgusted with your filth."

"I'm not talking about..." I cut off. I dared not say the name—old superstitions die hard.

A strange, bitter delight came to those ice-drilled eyes, and I felt a laughter like bubbling poison. "Oh, I think you are. He consumes your thoughts, makes you his day by day. Except he will never take you."

I struggled to keep my thoughts off Thomas, but his words bit deep. His finger bent into a claw as he dragged up in me all the passing glances of the past several days traveling, every time Thomas and I were close but did not touch, all the words I never spoke and never heard from him, he and Mahmoud practicing swordplay and the strength with which Thomas moved. And the Fire began to damp.

Now the leader's hand grasped as he came forward, fingers curving as though he held my heart in their long-boned cage. With one last flicker I felt the Fire: *No.*

My hand came up again, and the leader stopped as though he struck a wall. No fire this time, but lines of blood striped across my hand as though lashed by brambles. The blood beaded in the lacerations and began to run. But I felt no pain.

The five hissed again, a sharp indrawn breath. Another flash of lightning and pounding thunder, and they were gone. The booming thunder rolled slowly away, and the tapping faded down the street. I turned only long enough to see the five continuing up the road before I collapsed on the bed, fresh tears and exhaustion carrying me into oblivion again.

Chapter 2

I awoke to tapping again, this time the very natural tapping of knuckles on my wooden door. I blinked dry eyes; the sun was streaming in though I still heard a faint patter of rain. I picked up my head. The clouds were breaking, but not empty. Funny, I felt a little the same way.

"Rae-Anna?" Thomas called.

"I'm awake," I said. I wanted to bid him enter, but feared he wouldn't. The silence on the other side of the door stretched, and I sat up and dangled my feet off the edge of the bed. The scene from last night played again, but dimly. Not as a dream—it had been real, as far as "real" went in a spirit-infused sense. I shuddered to think of those men passing through town, or still in it somewhere. I wondered if I would recognize them again, if they would still be in the same form. I assumed they would not.

"Can I come in?"

I snapped out of my reverie. His voice was quiet, almost pleading. "One moment," I said as I hurriedly pulled on my stockings, made a vain attempt to smooth my hair which I assumed was wild. "Okay," I said. When he entered, I looked him up and down. His clothes were rumpled, his eyes dark and sunken, his hair in a sort of wave that broke upon the left shore of his head. I cleared my throat lightly as my hand fell from my own head. I wondered if the five men had visited him as well.

"Rough night?" I asked.

His lips quirked. "Does it show?" I tried a smile, but the thought of the pale faces coming after him worried me. "Mahmoud snores," he explained.

Thank Our Father. I laughed. "I never heard him on our road down here."

"Well, my fault I guess. Since he was staying just the one night I demanded he take the bed." He shrugged and looked away.

In the silence that followed, I almost told him what I had seen in the night, took a preparatory breath five or six times. But I struggled. We had shared much at the convent, and I knew—felt—he was committed to this journey. It seemed too soon, though, and I didn't want to test his commitment just now.

As it was, he spoke first. "Rae-Anna, you know what happened...with Judith." I folded my hands and waited as he continued. "I hoped...I thought when she was gone, when I knew I wouldn't have to face it again, that everything would be fine after that. But it's...I guess it's not that easy. When you reached out last night, I couldn't help..."

I was watching his lips as he spoke. He was still turned slightly away, and I suddenly noticed that certain words made the tip of his nose dip back—I guess as the skin stretched. He had a fine profile—strong angles, smooth skin. That messy hair, when placed properly, framed his face in a way that always drew me to him. Under the rumpled clothing, his muscles bunched as he folded his arms. His long fingers gripped his upper arm. I knew his hands were on the rough side—farmer's hands, after all—but I much preferred it to the soft, soggy hands of some of the monks or merchants I had met. And his eyes, flashing at me now—I would stare into those forever if I could, even when they seemed upset like they did now, if only to calm them again...

I stared at him in horror. "I'm so sorry," I said. "I don't know what happened..."

But it was too late, I could tell. Those beautiful lips pressed thin. "Mahmoud is gone already," he said, his voice flat. "We should eat, and then figure out what we're doing next."

"Thomas," I began, but he was already turning, and quickly left. The door banged shut. But in its wake I thought I heard a faint laughter, like bubbling. I trembled, squeezing my eyes shut against the memory. I would have to tell him, let him know there was some sort of power at work in this town. It seemed they were not gone, or at least the residue of them remained. It might be enough to pass from me to him, and he should know.

I tidied my appearance in a fog of whirling thoughts—about Thomas, myself, our situation—and by the time I was downstairs the memory of that laughter had faded. The memory of their visitation had not, though it still played in my mind as though on a dark mirror. But I had convinced myself they were not as important as I had thought, that perhaps they were gone again and there was no need to worry him yet. Not when we had other, more immediate concerns. He was right: we needed to find some kind of employment, and a place to stay.

His mood was still dark as we ate in silence. I might have enjoyed the food: the innkeeper kept a good table. But Thomas' angry silence and knowing the cost as we spent the last of Mahmoud's generosity weighed on me. The eggs went almost instantly cold in my mouth, the ham wouldn't break down as I chewed, and the bread turned back to flour in my mouth.

Finally, as the table cleared, Thomas sat back. "Any ideas?" he asked, though he still didn't look at me.

I swallowed, the last bite of bread dragging itself down my throat. "It depends on what the town has, if anything other than farmers and traders."

His eyes flickered. "Well, there were sheep on the other side. I saw them before the rain started."

I nodded once. "The Sisters taught me how to weave, at least a little. And I can clean," I added with a faint grin.

He didn't share my humor. "Hmm. And what should I do?"

"I don't know," I said. I was beginning to feel a faint flicker of anger. I had apologized, or tried to. "If you can't farm, could you guard...something?" I'll admit ignorance in what sort of employment you could get with a sword.

His eyes flicked to me, again with no mirth. "I'm not that good yet," he said. "And most things that needed guarding are caravans, so I would have to leave."

The anger in me wished he would, at this point. But my yearning for him cried out within me like a small child on a distant street. I wasn't sure which one showed on my face, or if they both did, but he wasn't looking anyway. I ran for the child to comfort it, wished I could throw myself into his arms and press tightly against him and never leave, to feel his skin against mine, to feel his lips...

I took a breath, stared at the table to study the grains of wood. When I looked up, his eyes lowered from mine. "I'm sorry," he said.

"Me too," I said quickly.

He shook his head. "Don't... People say that because they think they are expected to, and don't even know what they're apologizing for yet. Don't be like one of them."

I felt my back stiffen again. "I'm sorry that I wasn't listening—" I cut off when he made a disgusted grunt.

"Exactly. Let's go to the weaver's and see if you can work."

My eyes burned but I followed him. He had never been this difficult before—we had never been this difficult before. I thought back to the convent, that no matter what I was going through or when I learned what he was going through, we'd been able to talk. Always. I had thought that would be the worst of it, that nothing else we could go through would be as hard. Now we weren't even going through anything that hard, and he wouldn't speak to me—at least, not to explain himself. And I hadn't even told him about the night before, that we were on the verge of facing a new attack.

Maybe that's what would draw him back. Maybe if he knew we had a common battle he would come alongside again. "Thomas," I said tentatively as we made our way down the street. He didn't stop or turn, but he ducked his head a little. "Something happened last night," I continued. I kept my voice low; shops were opening and I didn't know who might overhear. "Five men came into the village. I think they're why we're here. They came into my room."

At this, he stopped suddenly and turned, eyes boring into mine. "How? When?"

"It was late, the storm was starting to break. They looked..." I trailed off and shuddered at the memory. "They are definitely evil," I said. "And in a flash of lightning somehow they appeared in the room behind me, instantly."

He frowned. "Probably a dream," he said.

My back went stiff again. "I know by now when I'm dreaming and when I'm not," I retorted. There was only that one time when I'd first woken up from receiving the Fire. But that was not this.

"What are you going to do about it, these men?"

I gaped. "Me?"

"Well they came into your room, not mine. I don't know how to use the Fire—you do remember that conversation, don't you? Or do you want me to try to kill them with this?" He shifted the hilt forward. "Guard...something, you said. Hopefully there's no storm when they come or they might just shift away to your room again."

"I thought we were in this together," I said.

He looked me up and down, and I saw some of the fight leave his eyes. "I did too."

We stood looking at each other for several long moments. "I don't know what I did wrong," I said softly.

It didn't have the effect I hoped; if anything, the fight returned worse. "Well when you figure it out, you can apologize for it." He turned on his heel and continued down the street.

"You've done some wrong things too," I said after him. He kept walking, stiffer now. "Thomas!" I called, eyes brimming. But he only turned and entered a shop, leaving me in the street.

Fear struck me then, and I looked wildly around. Those men could be anywhere, watching me, waiting for me to be alone again. Smiles surrounded me, and laughter echoed down the streets, but it mocked now. A few nearby looked at me in a strange, shocked way that I was not as happy as they were.

Slowly that fear hardened to anger. So. I was in this fight alone, then. I had fought the injustice of the Sisters on my own, fought most of the undead army on my own—the great big men around me only forcing the skeletons toward me to handle. I would handle this fight alone then, too.

I marched down the street and entered the shop, barely noticing the fabrics on display. Thomas waited quietly to one side when I entered. The shopkeeper was with a customer, settling on some skeins of wool. The keeper was a woman of middle height and weight, and her brown hair was pulled into a tight bun. A few graying wisps streaked it, and had pulled free around her ears. But she seemed kindly enough, and dressed modestly in a nut-brown dress. It was not a strong marker of her abilities, but stout enough. Certainly the cut was neater and color more vibrant than most I had seen outside.

I spared a quick glance at Thomas; he was shut tight, his arms folded across his chest. His gaze was firmly on the counter behind which the shopkeeper stood. I looked too, and froze.

Etched small on the side was the same mark that had been on the leader's staff, though not as intricate. Or perhaps it had faded some. But it was the same star, if the swirls were less complex. Had they marked this place somehow? Had they known I would end up here? Was this shopkeeper somehow related to those men, or their purpose?

"Maybe we shouldn't be here," I whispered.

I send you forth as sheep in the midst of wolves.

I sighed. He hadn't spoken to me like that since Holden. Figures he'd come back now. I kept still—Thomas had made no response, so I guess he still wanted me to fight alone—and waited for the keeper to be done.

As the other woman turned and left, sparing a small smile for me and a worried glance for Thomas, I stepped forward.

"What are you looking for?" she asked pleasantly.

I tried and failed to keep my eyes from darting to the symbol. If she knew where my glance went she didn't remark on it. "I was wondering if you had any employment for me," I said tentatively.

"We're going to be in town for some time, and we need work."

She looked at me critically. "What can you do?"

"I've learned much from the Sisters at Holden," I said. "I can do most, including weaving and crochet. I hadn't quite got the hang of knitting."

Her brows climbed as she nodded respectfully. "Easy to say," she said. "You came at a good time, though, with this wedding coming up. I'll start you cleaning and spinning, until I have time to see how you do everything else."

"Do you card it yourself?" I asked.

She gave a quick nod. "So you aren't entirely ignorant, though you could have learned as much at your mother's knee. I do; it relaxes me at the end of the day. Why did you leave the Sisters? Or were you thrown out?"

I smiled. "I left, with their blessings. Our Father's call on my life was different from theirs."

"Hmm. Are you staying at the inn? Or do you have family?"

"The inn." I faltered a moment. "I don't think we have enough to stay there long, though..."

Her face darkened a little. "Well, let's get you started and see by the end of the day. What about this one?" she asked, turning her gaze to Thomas.

"I'll find my own way," he said.

Her eyes darted to me as I grimaced, then back to him. "I don't doubt it lad, but I might be able to help if I knew what you could do."

"My father was a farmer."

"A lot of crop thieves in Holden?" she asked, raising a brow at his sword.

"No. This was...more recent. I can't use it well, yet."

"Do you want to?"

Thomas shrugged. I caught his glance, tried to plead with my eyes. He blinked and looked away. "I might need to."

She looked between us for an interminable spell. Finally she folded her arms. "I can't harbor fugitives," she said. When I made to speak she held up a finger to silence me. "Now, you don't look the type but they almost never do. If you're in earnest, I suggest you go to the Captain of the Guards and register yourself. He might have something for you. You"—she looked pointedly at me as her arms came down—"can find what you need back there." At her gesture, I made for the doorway at the back of the shop. When I glanced back at Thomas, he was already leaving. I watched the door shut behind him and swallowed

"Do you have a name?"

I startled. "Yes, sorry; I'm Rae-Anna. That was Thomas."

She nodded once. "Tabitha. Is he your brother?"

I smiled grimly. "After a fashion."

She glared a warning at me, then pointed silently again toward the back room. I went in. It was much as I expected after our conversation: neat, highly organized, efficient. The wall nearest was festooned with skeins, spools, and balls of thread and yarn by color and—I ran my fingers across one or two—material. I was surprised by the amount of cotton she had, and the vibrancy of some of the colors. For a small town she did very well for herself. Most was linen or wool.

In a separate corner stood the loom, a half-finished bolt of pale blue cloth there. Another corner, the spinning wheel, a basket of cleaned and carded wool beside it. Nearer a back door sat the ripple, break, scutching sword, and hackle for flax. There were no sheaves nearby and I wondered if she had them stored elsewhere, or only made it seasonally.

The final corner was mine. Wool was already sorted and stacked there with several tubs beside it. There was more wool waiting to be cleaned than was already clean, and nothing ready to spin, so I set to with the unwashed wool. The harshness of the lye bit at first, but I grew accustomed to it again, thankful at least that all the small cuts and breaks I had gained from scrubbing the dormitories was long gone.

After flinging the rinse water from my hands I peeked out the back door. In a bright patch in the yard behind the shop were the slats for drying. I moved the washed wool there and returned.

Tabitha was waiting when I entered. Her gaze took me in for a silent moment. "Do you have any questions?"

I could think of several, but none of them pertinent, so I shook my head. Her lips quirked into a grin. "Those will come," she said, and I cocked my head. She only smiled. A bell jingled from the front and she turned and left.

When I turned my back to start on the next batch of wool, I felt a creeping evil worm its way up my spine. I shuddered and turned suddenly as I heard the voices from the front room. They sounded pleasant enough to my ear, but in my heart they struck fear, and the flame flickered up again.

Chapter 3

With an inward groan I paused to listen. My heart beat fast. Through the doorway I could still hear the voices, though often the words themselves were indistinguishable. Still they sounded normal, pleasant even. A mere inquiry. I shook my head and turned back toward the wool. But I couldn't make myself step away. The fear on my spine gripped now, and I couldn't break free. There was something familiar about the touch, and I thought instantly of the night before.

I turned and peeked out. Tabitha's back was toward me as she spoke with three men—one was young, perhaps only a year or two older than Thomas. The two behind him were older but not fatherly. Yet there was an air about them, a gravitas, that captured my attention.

"I don't doubt your speed, Mistress," the youngest was saying with a laugh. "Or your skill. I'm not checking to see if it will be done in time. I just want to see it. Am I not allowed to be curious?"

At those words, one of the elders looked directly at me and the fear that held my spine reached an icy finger toward my heart. The flame rose up as a shield, and the finger recoiled.

I saw a faint spark in the man's eye, and suddenly realized everyone had turned to look at me. Tabitha's frown was deep; the others were merely curious.

"She's new," said the youngest, a playful glint in his eye.

"And meant to be working," Tabitha said quietly but with force.

"You must forgive her," he continued. "I am not upset to look at one so fair. I would have regretted the missed opportunity."

I flushed, and ducked my head. "Forgive me, Mistress," I said. "I thought I recognized something. A voice."

I looked up as the elder's gaze bored a little deeper into mine. He turned, and something flashed near his neck—a pendant hung there, and I stifled a gasp as I recognized the pattern from the staff. This one was a perfect replica, crisp and unfaded. As I looked up, his eyes grew briefly dark, glittering with shards of ice.

"I-I'm sorry," I stammered. But even as I backed away a step, something in me hardened. "These men...who are they?"

"Patrons of my shop," Tabitha said, louder and firmer.

I glanced between the two elders. The second seemed strangely benign—was he one of the five? Even if so, where were the other three? I felt a crawling again, worried they might be creeping up behind me. But I had nothing certain. "That one," I said as I pointed. "I've met him before. I would have nothing to do with him, if I could."

I expected anger, fear—not laughter. All three men laughed, and even Tabitha quirked another smile, though it soon disappeared. "Wouldn't you?" she said.

The youngest spoke again. "I'm sorry you feel that way. I have known these two all my life. Fair as you are, maiden, I trust them more than you." He said the last gently enough, and turned to

Tabitha. "It is always entertaining to visit your shop," he said generously. "And do please forgive her; I am sure none of us have taken offense. May I see the dress, though?"

Tabitha turned away from me, and I shrunk deeper into the back room. "It is not proper, your lordship, to see the wedding dress before the day comes, and I think you know that."

My heart fell into my stomach as the icy hand slid down my spine again. That young man must be the town's mayor—and the strange men were advisors or friends of some kind. What new danger had I gotten myself into? What kind of danger threatened the mayor, or the town?

I returned to the wool almost numbly and continued my work. As I heard the door shut faintly at the front of the shop, the fear drained away entirely, not leaving even a residue. I stared at the wall while I worked the wool in the lye and rung it, and feared. But the Fire in me remained silent, though present. It had protected me, I knew, and more than once from whatever insidious attack that man was capable of. And yet it had let me feel the fear, and remained silent now when I needed to know what was expected of me. It occurred to me how little I still understood.

"If you plan on working here," Tabitha said suddenly; I turned with a yelp. "You can do best by not accusing the mayor—or any customer for that matter—of distrust. I know which customers to distrust, and will take care of them myself."

I nodded. "I apologize," I said. "I had seen a mark on his medallion—a sort of scrollwork star." I looked at her closely to see if she reacted. She didn't. "I had seen another carrying the same symbol, using it to work some evil."

She arched an eyebrow. "Perhaps you are right," she said. "Perhaps the Sisterhood has over-sensitized you. While you are here, though, you will clean wool and keep your comments to yourself."

"Yes, mistress." She stared at me a moment longer until I returned to the work, then left.

Be not afraid, but speak, and hold not thy peace: for I am with thee, and no man shall set on thee to hurt thee.

There was good news, I guess.

The rest of the day went well enough. I worried occasionally about Thomas, worried more often what specifically he saw I did wrong. But it seemed there were no specific words from Our Father to answer either of those. Tabitha would come to the back every now and again, sometimes to retrieve bolts of cloth or thread or yarn. Other times the shop was empty and she would do a little carding, but always in silence.

The sound of ringing bells wafted through the town, the first familiar thing since leaving Holden. Tabitha came to the back of the shop one more. "I'm going out for a moment, but the shop will be closed. Do you know how to break flax?" I nodded. She gestured to a ladder near where I stood. "Bundles are up there. Keep busy until I get back." I nodded again, and she left.

It wasn't until I was on my way back down the ladder after gathering a half-hour's work that I was surprised she trusted me alone in her shop. How easy might it be to take some of the more expensive bolts and go out the back door?

I shrugged. Not that I had any intention of doing so. I set to work with the break. It had been some time since I had worked things such as these. I didn't realize how much I missed the simple tasks. Even the sounds, the soft clatter as the break came together, the squeezing of the stalks of flax. Pith and odd grassy bits collected beneath the break in a small pile. I worked it end to end and back, making it supple as possible. She would want to make good linen, I could tell already.

I startled when the door beside me suddenly opened; I hadn't thought someone could open it from outside. Tabitha entered, a small woven basket tucked in her arm. She looked me up and down, glanced at the finished knots I had made. I think I saw a bit of respect gleam in her eye.

"Come and eat," she said.

I followed her to a small table. She set out thick slices of bread as trenchers, then piled them with slices of ham and cheese. She pulled a crock from the basket, and when she opened the lid I could smell lentils. She handed me a wooden spoon.

"If you came from the Sisters, perhaps you should offer the prayer," she said.

I agreed, offering a quick but proper grace, and we set to. It was warm and filling, and we ate quietly for a time. As we finished the last of the meat and cheese and started on the trenchers, she settled back.

"Now," she said, and her gaze offered no escape. "Tell me about yourself, and why you are here."

I took a breath, but held it a moment. *Be not afraid, but speak.* I let my breath out in a rush, and began to tell her. I did not give her details of the attacks at Holden, just that there was some evil I had fought. It helped she asked for a prayer, but I didn't know how much she knew or believed, and didn't want to frighten her off.

"And Thomas?" she asked when I had finished. "After what fashion is he your brother?"

I gave a rueful smile. "In The Beloved," I admitted. "We share common faith, that's all." I didn't mean for as much bitterness to creep into that last part. Maybe I did.

She arched an eyebrow. "Truly?"

I considered a moment, remembered his tightly-folded arms, his swift departure. "I am perfectly certain."

She gave some sort of half-smile that I couldn't interpret. "Well, you've worked hard today already. I don't want to leave you uncertain, so if you continue as you have the rest of the day I'll give you a pallet for tonight." She cocked her head a moment. "Unless you don't want it, now."

I didn't know what to say. We needed a place. The symbol worried me, but I didn't want to mention it directly. Not after my outburst earlier. But if she was aware of it, was part of it, why would she offer me room?

My mind worked frantically. "Your husband won't mind?" I asked, thinking of the next-best possible reason for hesitating.

But when the pain flashed across her face, I knew it was not next-best. "No, child, he won't mind," she said quietly. My hand reached out, but fell short.

Be. Not. Afraid. The flame was nearly an ember, struggling against the extinguishing winds of my doubt.

"I'm so sorry," I said. "It was foolish of me to say—and a deception. There was a symbol etched on your counter, I saw it when Thomas and I first came in. I fear for what it might mean."

She studied me a moment, confused. Suddenly her eyes lit up. "Oh, that. I'm sorry you feared for nothing. That board was given to me, when my husband and I were just starting this shop, to replace a dilapidated one. I assumed that was some sort of Master Carpenter's mark. What is it, if not?"

I thought a moment. "I'm not sure," I said baldly. "Perhaps it is his mark, but there's still an innocent explanation for it. Many people ignorantly follow gods they don't know, I suppose, and even no longer worship."

"And many people falsely accused on those exact grounds." She looked aside. "Did you know there were many who accused me of the same, when my husband died? Of course you wouldn't. But they thought I spurned Our Father by staying in business. I should have fallen in service to another, I guess, or lived off widow's charity." She shook her head minutely. "Pavel felt differently, when he lived. It was he who taught me to weave." She smirked. "Not The Liar, despite the accusations. Some of them, anyway. The rest of the town did everything to help me. Do you think I would have prospered if The Liar benefited me?"

I realized she was asking earnestly. I gaped a moment—who was I to teach, half her age and not a true Sister? Well, not ordained by the Order, I suppose. I closed my mouth and considered a moment. "Man looketh on the outward appearance," I said slowly. I fixed her gaze. "Whether you prospered or not has no bearing, I think. Our Father blesses the just and the unjust. But in the half-day I've known you, you have been most just toward me. And I know, at least, I am not come from The Liar," I finished with a smile.

Her grin was tighter, grimmer. "I think you speak truthfully, though I had hoped...it would be much easier if it were the other way."

I laughed. "Easier for those who prosper; unbearable for those who do not, though," I said, gesturing to my simple dress, calling attention to my need for her—or someone's—charity.

Her smile now was genuine and full. "I think it will be good for you to be here, and now I give you my pallet without reservation."

"And I accept," I said. A thought flashed through my mind. "What of...Thomas?"

She looked at me askance. "You share only your faith?"

I slumped. "I think so."

I saw mirrored in her eyes some of the pain I felt. "I cannot say all, child," she said. "But I think you should not be so hopeless."

"I don't want to be," I said miserably. "A week ago, I was not. Now..."

"If I know men," she said with a meaningful glance, "he'll be back. And you will work it out."

I couldn't tell if her confidence was inspiring, misguided, or I only wished it were true. Visions of the morning passed through my mind again, when my eyes were wandering over him in ways I had never permitted myself before. The Order prevented me at first, then the novelty and demands of our travels kept me focused. I had longed to look at him in that way for months. In truth, I had seen him a few times in the village before even departing for the convent. Back then, my curse kept me from looking at any man too long for fear he would fall into temptation because of me.

Tabitha rose and cleared the table, and when she returned to the front, I returned to my work. My mind stayed on Thomas. I couldn't understand him. We had touched before, lovingly; had admitted to things we felt. I could maybe understand why I wouldn't be allowed to touch him now—at least, not without warning. So I had contented myself with looking. I thought he would appreciate it. Instead he seemed angrier about that. Well, about my distraction, yes; but when he found out why... Or when I explained that something was going on in this town, that evil was here, that appeased him less!

I shook my head to myself. I had work to do, and nothing could be resolved through one-sided conversation. I did hope Tabitha was right, at least that he would come back. Whether or not we worked it out was not entirely dependent on me.

She closed the shop by supper, and we ate in silence. Thomas had not returned. Afterward, she carded while I stood at the spinning wheel. She checked my thread every now and again, but I had not forgotten so much by then. She lit a few rushlights as the windows grew dark, but we did not work much longer.

"Tomorrow we'll spin some thicker yarns," she said. "With winter coming we'll sell more of those. Perhaps you can crochet some hoods, though I may teach you some knitting—most have come to expect knit woolens from me. You can do that, though?" I nodded. "Good. As I said, your pallet is up that ladder, and there is a blanket or two you can use if you need." She observed me a moment as I hesitated. "Perhaps tomorrow you might fetch our lunch, if you want to inquire about your brother."

I smiled, only partly hollow. By now I assumed him gone, if not physically at least we would not be what we were. I knew I was being a little dramatic, but it is no small thing to have at least a little reassurance when your thoughts turn dark. The fact he had not returned to the shop—even just to let me know what work he had found—spoke far louder than anything Tabitha could say.

I climbed the ladder. The pallet was straw tick, but not terribly lumpy, and the blankets were indeed warm. The walls were not thick, and I thought perhaps the chinking had not been tended in some time—it was primarily a storage place, not meant to spend a length of time in and certainly not at night. But I recalled the far-colder nights at the convent and fell sound asleep.

I dreamed of the Sisters' faces swirling around me, sometimes sad, sometimes angry, rarely happy. Thomas was tapping at the window and then was suddenly whisked away. A pair of birds sat on a branch and one fell suddenly from a stone slung by a child. The rock and the bird thumped when they hit the ground, while the second bird merely watched. The little child, a girl, plucked the feathers in one swipe and set it over a fire. The fire rose, raging, nearly consuming the hearth and the little girl.

Thomas was tapping at the window again, face streaked in blood. I reached for him, saw the same stripes of blood on my hands. But I could not reach him. I struggled as though in a pit of thick mud as he continued to tap. But instead of a fingernail on glass it sounded like an iron-capped walking stick approaching on a cobblestone street.

I gasped, recognizing the sound, but unable to awake. The tapping grew closer; Thomas' eyes widened in horror and he disappeared from the window. The pale, maggot-white face replaced it, large, sharp teeth bared as he laughed. He held up a torch that raged.

I awoke in the darkness as the Fire raged inside me, and I lay gasping in sweat. There were furtive noises from below, and pale firelight wavered through the hole and into my little room. I imagined Thomas tapping at the window and rushed to the trapdoor and the ladder. I looked through the hole. There was a figure below, hooded, shielding a rushlight as they moved through the room. The back door was open.

"Thomas?" I called softly.

The figure paused, and the hood-opening cast around the room. I called again, and he looked up.

It was not Thomas. It was no one I had seen before. My voice stuck in my throat, not sure what to do. It had to be an intruder, but Tabitha should have locked the door.

He was smiling, but it turned my stomach. There was nothing behind the smile, not familiarity or pleasance—an entirely hollow smile below hollow eyes. And not only nothing, but an emptiness so vast it threatened to suck in everything around it and still not be satiated.

I thought I saw a brief flicker in those eyes, a sparkling like stars in a void. He cast down the rushlight, into the midst of my knotted flax. I squinted as they lit furiously—far faster than they should have. When I could see again, the figure was gone and the door was shut. The fire still raged.

"Tabitha!" I called loudly, hurrying down the ladder. I picked up one of the rinsing tubs and dashed it on the flax. Tabitha entered as I picked up the next one.

"What's happening?" she demanded. I poured that tub on the flames as well; they damped, but were not yet extinguished, and burned with a greater heat than they had before. I looked around for another source of water. The wood flooring began to crackle, now.

Tabitha rushed over with a bolt of cloth in her hands. She began to beat the flames. I joined her, but suddenly mine caught and I tossed burning bits of cloth around the room. I watched in horror as the scattered embers burst suddenly into intense flame.

Tabitha stood, her eyes darting. They fixed on me, and the questions and pain burned bright in them. I gaped, unable to offer an answer or explanation.

...who through faith quenched the violence of fire...

I breathed out a quick prayer, reaching inside to feel the Sacred Fire. It surged upward, met me, and I felt a cooling balm like water cascade down my head. The flames in the room struggled and I felt desperate hate from them, then they winked out all at once and the room was dark.

Chapter 4

We stood in the darkness for several long moments, with only the sound of our breathing. An acrid smell still clung to the air. I sneezed.

"Does this happen around you a lot?" Tabitha asked quietly.

"Only recently," I said.

"How did the fire start?"

"Someone came in the back door. I didn't recognize him. But he was hooded like the evil men I had seen before. He lit it."

Her foot scraped the floor as she stepped away. A small light flared as she lit another rush. Her eyes were troubled as she looked around, then to me. "These evil men who you say are connected to the mayor?"

"I'm not certain they are connected," I replied. "They bore the same symbol, but so does your shop counter."

She grunted at that. "Makes me wonder," she muttered. She picked up the charred flax—what had not become ash—and turned it over in her hand. "You really had done a good job with this," she said. She tossed it in the empty tub.

"You're taking this rather in stride," I said.

"Huh." She smirked at me. "I was the heretic who kept her own shop open after her husband died. It's not the first time someone tried to burn it down."

"I think this is a little different," I said carefully. I wanted to be honest with her, but I also didn't want to be told to leave. But, for her safety...

She gazed flatly at me. "I'm trying to ignore that, and focus on the fact you put out fires that were rapidly spreading." She gave a half-hearted smile. "And that could be very good to have around." She sighed with one more glance around the room. "Everything else seems in order. Go back to sleep; we've work to do tomorrow."

She reached out and gave my shoulder a squeeze. I waited for her to depart, the little wavering globe of light going with her. In the darkness I reached inside again, felt the glow of the Fire there. *I'm so sorry.* I had been ignoring it for so long. I hadn't realized I had been trying to slip into a normal life again, so soon after all it had done for me. My life had never been normal, though, not in the village, not in the convent. It didn't make me any happier to realize that, too; for a moment it made it worse and I felt my mouth twist bitterly. But then I wondered what I meant by "normal"—if anyone had a "normal" life. From the outside, perhaps, or when we considered it all together. But in the day-by-day, did anyone feel their life was "normal"?

I climbed the ladder wearily, and laid down again on the pallet. Though my limbs felt like water my mind was on edge. More than once I thought I heard the tapping either approaching or retreating. I thought I saw a faint glow from the hole and feared the man had returned. After staring at it wide-eyed for long moments, I realized it was the dawn making its way through the windows and the shop.

I must have slept a little, but it didn't feel like it. I heard movement below, Tabitha readying the shop, and I rose.

As I stepped off the last rung, Tabitha poked her head around the corner. "I've sent for a carpenter," she said. She nodded toward the back door. "High time to be able to bolt that, I think. And the smell is gone." She gazed meaningfully at me as I sniffed. She was right; the charred scent that should have clung for perhaps weeks was gone. As I glanced around the room, I noticed there was no charred wood where the flames had been. I looked at her and shrugged. I could no more explain it than she could—at least, not beyond what I already had.

I followed Tabitha into the front. She was laying out strips of linen dyed various colors. "I was surprised to see you couldn't bolt that door before," I said.

"It hadn't been that kind of village, before," she replied. "Oh they thought I was a heretic, but they never went behind my back. I guess with all these come in for the wedding..." She left the rest unsaid, but I didn't think it was a random traveler. I found myself looking at the mark on her counter, wondering what it meant. Was that why the mayor and his "friends" came to this shop? Did they expect something from her—and, if they did, and she didn't give it, what might that mean?

"Are there any other seamstresses or weavers in town?" I asked.

Tabitha chuckled. "Yes, there's another, but..." She smiled and shook her head. "He only serves the non-heretics." She winked at me, then went past and into the back. I followed. Tabitha went to a closet next to the ladder and pulled out a folding screen and set it between her and the front, then slid out a wooden framework over which she had begun making a dress. So far the skirts were mostly arranged, though I could tell they hadn't been cut yet. It looked elaborate, far more elaborate than any of her other articles... Of course.

"The wedding dress," I said. She hummed as she smiled, settling herself on a stool as she began to work the fabric. "It's beautiful," I continued. I tried to imagine the build of the woman who would wear it. She would not be slim with that waist, and yet the skirts alone still bespoke a daintiness I didn't have and would never attain with a life on the road. I wasn't sure why that mattered to me.

I shook my head and retrieved more bundles of flax. "Just to replace what we lost yesterday?" I offered. "It shouldn't take me long."

"Go ahead," she agreed. We worked silently for a time, until the door bell tinkled from the front.

"Miss Tabitha?" a deep voice called.

"The carpenter," she said to me, before calling: "back here!"

I kept an eye on the doorway a moment, catching sight of the aging man who came through. He was not fat, but he had a little bit of a waddle. He dressed simply enough in brown shirt and pants. He carried a sort of box in one hand, and I saw tools of various handles protruding. In his other he carried one plank of wood. He paused when he saw me.

"Henri, this is Rae-Anna," Tabitha introduced with a wave of her hand. "Don't worry about her."

"Of course not," he rumbled, though he seemed as though he did worry. Tabitha busied herself with the dress, and after a moment Henri continued his gait to the back door. He leaned the timber against the frame and grasped the handle. He was about to pull it, but noticed the jamb. He turned to Tabitha. "Why'd you have this open outward?" he asked gruffly.

She glanced at him. "I didn't build it, Henri," she said patiently. I fought back a grin, hiding it the moment before Henri turned on me.

And yet I couldn't help myself as he stared at me.

"I didn't build it either," I said as seriously as I could.

I jumped as the box crashed to the floor, the tools rattling inside. "Fit for a king's jester," Henri mumbled, though I felt no harm in him. I glanced at Tabitha who only raised an eyebrow and smiled. "I'll need to go get a different bracket," Henri said.

A thought struck me as he started to leave, and I hurried after him. "Henri," I called out as he neared the door. He turned, glowering. It seemed he was just like that. "Is this a carpenter's mark that you know?" I asked, pointing to the faded symbol.

He seemed reluctant to take his eyes off me, as though I might be poking more fun at him. But when he looked, after a moment's study he paled, then went red. "I'm an honest man," he said, looking up. "I do my work. And you young...women...only seem to jest and prod."

"Henri, we meant nothing by it," I said. "But you did ask a kind of silly question."

He grumbled. "A man doesn't talk and you say he's too quiet; he starts talking and you say he's silly. 'Twas merely a thought that foolishly came out, I'm sorry." He made an elaborate bow and turned to leave.

"Henri," I pleaded. He stopped but didn't turn. "You're absolutely right, and I'm very sorry. I'm sure Tabitha would be too." He glanced over his shoulder with a raised eyebrow. Maybe she wouldn't be; he knew her probably better than I. "But this is—it might be very important, if you know this symbol."

He turned halfway, but did not look at the counter again. When he spoke, his voice had lost all of its bluster. "If you don't know it, lady, then I should not tell you. It might be taken wrong, by the wrong people. Don't prod!"

He left hurriedly, and I returned to the back. It was perhaps the worst answer he could have given. All I knew was it was something like I feared, but nothing of what it was about. Was it some sort of signal?

Tabitha was tucking something away when I looked up, I couldn't tell what. But distracted as I was I merely went back to work. She kept humming, some tune I vaguely remembered from a festival day back in Holden.

Henri returned a little later, and the three of us worked without talking most of the morning. He was truly a Master, working with an efficiency I admired. Never a wrong move or misplaced gesture, and he didn't even bother to test the quality when he was done. He merely thunked the bar across the door, turned, and thanked Tabitha. She smiled and paid him along with her own thanks, and he was gone.

"And now, lunch," she said. "Despite my confidence before the mayor yesterday, I am further behind than I would like on this dress. Here." She handed me the little bag of coins out of which she'd just paid Henri. "Just on the other side of the inn is a seller, Jannis. Tell him it's for me and he'll give you what you need. And pay what he asks; he and I worked it out long ago."

I left with only a vague smile. She never asked what I chased after Henri for, and I never mentioned it. She had given her explanation, and I doubted with further prodding she would change it—even if it were false. Besides, I still didn't have any clear idea what it was. That it worried him so also worried me, and yet it fit. If it did belong to those men, or some society they belonged to, of course it was gravely evil. But why were they such close friends of the mayor? Was it a society, or was it only them?

I passed the inn, saw Jannis' storefront. His was openly on the street, three tables set in a circle with goods laid out on it. He was with another, so I waited while I looked over what he had. I didn't know if Tabitha ever intended to pay me in coin, or just give me the room—not that I would be ungrateful. But if I ever wanted to buy something for myself...

The customer turned and I stepped aside to clear his path with a mumbled greeting, eyes still on the red and golden apples. When he didn't move, I finally looked at him.

"Oh! Thomas!" Happiness, anger, puzzlement, and attraction all danced a whirling jig through me. His own features seemed to go from displeasure to amusement. I latched on to that, at least at first. "I didn't...I was looking at the apples, I didn't expect you here. Where..." The anger and puzzlement crept back in. "Where have you been?"

"Working," he said. "Haven't you?"

"Yes, of course. And she's letting me stay in her loft. You can stay there too..." I trailed off as his lips compressed.

"I don't think that would be a good idea," he said.

My heart fell. "Because you're still angry with me?" I said. I couldn't help it. As soon as it left my mouth, I worried I should have made it my fault—it was, in a way, though I still hadn't figured out what precisely I had done.

"No," he said softly. I knew immediately what he meant by the tone. There were only a few, very particular times he had spoken to me in that tone. And my heart soared.

But I knew I still shouldn't try to touch him. I had never fought so hard to remain still, and I gripped my hands together tightly. "Please come by tonight," I said. "I need to talk to you."

He nodded. "I will. After supper, Mr. Messick is done with me for the day."

"Is it good work? Is he treating you well?"

His lips went thin again. I couldn't help watching them, but I tried to listen too. "We can talk tonight," he said finally. "It's fine," he continued quickly as my eyes flashed to his. "Yes, he does. But...well, we can talk tonight." He smiled, and for the briefest of moments I saw him the way we were before the fire came to me.

I smiled in return. "Okay," I said. "That sounds...I'll like that very much. And I'll be sure to listen, this time."

"Well," he said, "we'll have to talk about that, too. But I have to go; Mr. Messick will start to wonder if I'm coming back."

His first words jolted me, though he hadn't said it harshly. And I knew we would have to talk about it, I just didn't expect him to be so forthright with it. "Okay," I said. And he left.

I turned to Jannis, who politely acted as though he hadn't heard any of it. "For Tabitha, at—" But Jannis began gathering food immediately and piling it into a basket. It looked the same as the one Tabitha had yesterday and I wondered if he had somehow gotten it back. As he handed it to me, I realized he could have come to the shop towards the end of the day—I was rarely in the front and didn't know who came in or not.

"Tuppence," he said. My eyebrows lifted. I had thought, when Tabitha warned me not to haggle, it would be steep. For me alone it would have been, true—I wouldn't make twice that in a day. But for Tabitha, and food enough for both of us...I handed over the coins, thanked him, and left.

"Rae-Anna?" she called from the back when I entered the shop.

"Yes," I replied; I had come in from the front, assuming the back door would still be barred.

"Give me a moment, please," she said.

I waited, brows furrowed as I listened to the thumps and scrapes coming from the back. It was not my place, and likely not my concern, but she had not struck me as the secretive kind before. Soon enough her head poked around the corner and she waved me back. We began setting the table.

"Did you see Thomas?" she asked.

I startled, glancing at her, at her knowing smile. "You knew he would be there," I said.

She shrugged. "It's a small enough village," she said. "I asked around a little when I went yesterday, was told he had come across one Mr. Messick who I know..." She tilted her hand. "Reasonably well. I thought you might meet him there." She handed out her utensils again and we sat. "Are you still worried about him?"

"I suppose not," I said. "At least, not about that."

She waited for grace, and to start eating. "What is the worry, then?" she asked.

"I don't know yet," I said. It was mostly true—I didn't know enough to converse about it. "He said he would come by tonight, after supper? So we could talk."

"Good!" she said with a wide grin.

The rest of the afternoon dragged on, and then suddenly we were eating supper. I don't even remember what we talked about. I was listening for the door, even though he had said "after." Maybe Mr. Messick ate dinner early.

Tabitha smiled as she cleaned up as though she knew all this was going on. Probably she did. She seemed to have a grasp of things I didn't realize. It made me feel a little foolish for it, but I couldn't help myself anyway. She left, then, going to her own room I supposed.

I sat in the silence, in the light of the single rush, trying not to count my breaths. Some type of celebration went by the shop outside, not entirely drunken. A dog barked somewhere else. Just as I realized I could use the time to pray, I heard the door open and the little bell tinkle. I rose and went to the front. For a brief moment, I feared it would not be Thomas—that another hooded man would come to visit. But then I came around the doorway and there he was.

He stood stiffly, and his eyes were blank, though somewhat affixed to the strange symbol on the counter. I stopped. Something was wrong. I felt a strange charge in the air. "Thomas?" I called quietly.

His eyes didn't move, didn't look at me. "I'm sorry. I don't think talking will solve anything," he said. His voice was flat, wooden. "I just came to tell you that. I can't live this life you're trying to drag me into."

My heart quailed, and yet the Fire in me bolstered me like someone holding me up. "Thomas, you know it was always your choice."

His eyes flickered then as though he tried to move them but was unable. "That's what manipulators say, isn't it." This time his voice had an odd dual quality, as though two voices spoke at once. "Leave me alone!"

I studied him. That sounded like his own voice, well enough, and yet...

There was a flicker of movement outside, but in the darkness I couldn't see what it was. Thomas suddenly turned and the bell tinkled again as he left. And I could swear, just as the door swung shut, there was the corner of a swirling cloak out in the street as Thomas' boots tapped away. And, with the tapping, now a sound of metal clattering faintly.

Tabitha came almost immediately out of her room. "What happened? Did he leave so soon?"

I continued looking at the door. "I think we need to find out everything we can about that symbol," I said. "And I need to meet the Mayor's friends."

Chapter 5

"**B**ut if you go back to Henri, won't he foist you off like he did before?"

Tabitha asked a legitimate question, and I continued spinning the yarn while I considered it. We had gone back to work, now that our evening was free again. And I had forgotten how the wheel helped me think. Tabitha carded, silently waiting.

"Maybe I don't start with him," I mused. "He said if I didn't know, he was not one to tell me. If I can uncover a few details about it first, make it seem like I already know a little bit, he'll reveal the rest."

She nodded. "Perhaps, though he can sit like a boulder in a hole once he's made up his mind. So, where do you start, then?"

Where indeed. "What about the Mayor?"

She barked a short laugh. "We're a small enough village, but you wouldn't know it to talk to him. If he doesn't come to you, you don't talk to him."

"Can't someone petition to talk to him, if it was something important? Or aren't there, I don't know...councils or something he attends?"

It was her turn to consider. The wheel creaked once; it would need tallow soon. "Councils are always held in his residence," she said finally. "And only those invited are permitted. But the next isn't scheduled until after the wedding. Petitions, though..." She shook her head. "Again with the wedding he's probably quite distracted. You could send a request, I guess. I assume you want to start looking into this sooner, though."

"Very much so." We continued, the wheel silent again. "I wonder... If I did see one of the mayor's friends outside, did he intercept Thomas somehow? Or had he known he would be coming to me? How well do you know Mr. Messick? Who is he?"

"I've met him once or twice, when he used to get around. I was never entirely clear who he was, except someone very important. My husband and I weren't from here, originally; we came here when a plague came through our village to the south. But when we did, we had to meet Mr. Messick shortly after we arrived and when we intended to stay here."

"Was he the mayor, back then?"

"No, the mayor came from a different line. It was the current mayor's predecessor when we arrived, and while he didn't exactly defer to Mr. Messick..." She paused a moment as she began clearing the combs. "I got the sense the mayor never quite contradicted him either." She snagged a new batch of wool and began again.

"Would I be able to see him?" I asked.

She gave a little half-smile. "We might be able to arrange something. Oddly, he is a little more attainable than the mayor. I think he likes the company. I'll see if I can send a message in the morning."

The night was quiet, at least externally. Internally, I worried about Thomas until I managed to fall asleep, and again several times when

I awoke through the night. He had to have been in some kind of thrall, but what kind? Was he still in it? I had to think he would come back to me as soon as the thralldom ended. And when had he gotten it? Had he been intercepted? Or was there something at this Mr. Messick's house? What if Messick himself did it? Tabitha didn't seem to think of him that way, but I still only had her word that the symbol on her counter didn't hold her under some sway either. Was this all some elaborate trap?

I awoke finally to a rooster crowing in the village, not well-rested, but the urgency I felt propelled me to my feet and down the ladder. No sooner had I landed and rubbed the last sleep from my eyes when the front bell tinkled. I blinked owlishly; surely she had no customers so early.

I wandered to the front. I froze seeing the couple standing there, then quickly tried to smooth my hair—I assume in vain. They weren't so much looking at me anyway. Tabitha still had not emerged from her room.

"Yes?" I asked.

Their gazes broke from each other and spun to face me. The girl giggled behind her hand as the man gave a short chuckle. "We need a dress," he said loudly. He did not seem drunk, just very…outgoing.

I cleared my throat quietly. I usually had at least a swallow of water before needing to talk to anyone. But I moved to the counter. Where was Tabitha? "What kind of dress?" I asked. I tried to find something to write with—it would not be much but the Sisters had taught me some.

"A wedding dress, of course!" he boomed. The girl dissolved in more giggles.

I looked them over. It was not my place, but… Well, it was not my place. "Congratulations!" I said in as much joy as I could muster. It was still early. "What materials did you want?"

"The best you have, naturally," he said. He gazed at her. "Something fitting for the most beautiful woman in Aurden, and all the countryside around."

She blushed deeply. "I am not," she said, but of course there was no actual fight in it. She was not unattractive, I thought harshly. I smiled.

"Of course," I said. "Although the beauty of the dress is often in the cut, and not the material. How it's made, you might say. But the more complex the more time it takes to make. When is the wedding?"

He leaned close, conspiratorially. "We thought before the mayor's wedding, while the bunting is still up," he said. "That way we can pretend it's for us."

He might have seen my smile fade if he hadn't immediately turned his gaze to his fiancée as she giggled again. I jammed one of my fingers against the counter to ground myself. It was not my place. "I'll have to see with the seamstress, Tabitha; she knows her schedule."

"Well where is she? Bring her out," he boomed again, with a hearty laugh. His fiancée took a playful swipe at him, then crammed herself into his side as if to never leave. He bent down and kissed her hard on the mouth. I lowered my eyes, not refraining to clear my throat.

"Stop," she said finally, though huskily this time. She looked somewhat embarrassed, though not as mortified as I felt. He only laughed again.

"We can, if you want, take the measurements until Tabitha arrives," I said.

"I was told you could figure that out just by looking at her," he said, his eyes twinkling.

To his credit, she was as inappropriately dressed as to nearly be able to. "I am not the seamstress," I reiterated. "But if I give her your requirements and measurements she can begin work without at first seeing you."

"Fine. Let's get started then!" He looked at me as though expecting me to begin to measure her right then and there.

My throat would be so clear as to be see-through by the time I finished with this lout. "Stay right here, then, and we'll go to the back."

"I can come too," he said as I turned to leave. I turned back and stared hard at him.

"Measuring for a dress can become int—" I didn't want to say 'intimate' for fear of his response. "Inappropriate for onlookers," I finished instead.

The look of pure lasciviousness that flashed through his eyes as she began to disentangle herself from him made me shiver. I managed to hold my smile until she came with me and went to the back. I had her step up onto the small platform near the center of the room where Tabitha would stand dresses to make the final adjustments. As she disrobed to her shift, I searched quickly for measuring and writing implements. I had only basic knowledge of measuring—enough, I thought, to get Tabitha started if she would have the time.

When I finally found what I needed and turned back, the young woman was glaring playfully. I turned back and saw the man had managed to position himself to see through the door, though he had to bend nearly entirely over the counter to do so.

I ground my teeth and went to the closet, pulling out the folding screens and roughly setting them up. The girl had enough sense, at least, to look chastened as I did it. I held back a sigh and began measuring.

"You mustn't think too harshly of him," she said quietly as I worked.

I thought I must. "Left arm," I said. She lifted it dutifully.

"You know how men are," she continued. "And that one. He could have his pick, you know."

"Hold this here." I pressed the line against her armpit and let it fall to her ankle. How men are. Some of them, anyway.

"He's strong, well-liked in town. Everyone looks up to him, I'm told. I don't mind looking up to him myself," she added with a giggle. She stood on tiptoe to peek over the screen. I waited to take the measurement until she finally plonked back down onto her heels. She heaved a gusty sigh. "And when he looks at me... I could hardly believe it when he came to my father last week to court me."

I bruised the tip of the quill as I looked up at her. "Last week?"

She looked down at me in hurt surprise. "It's not like I had never heard of him before that. Everyone in town knows him. I had been waiting for him, actually."

My eyes narrowed a fraction. "Waiting for him, how? Was he promised to you already?"

"Oh no, not at all. He was distracted by some of the other ladies in town, is all. But I knew they would never be good for him. I just needed to wait for him to realize it. And then he did!" Her eyes sparkled like dawn stars, and I could nearly see his figure reflected in them. It was all she saw.

I had no idea where Tabitha kept the trimming instruments for her quill. I finished the measurements quickly, committing the last few numbers to memory. I would not be able to keep my mouth shut for much longer, and it was not my place. Nor would she have any reason to take my advice.

She dressed as I returned the implements, and I escorted her out. The girl—I had never bothered to learn either of their names, but assumed they would be back—re-glued herself to the man's side. I didn't know if Tabitha required some sort of first payment, so I asked a shilling, for my efforts if nothing else, and they departed.

The shop was silent, and the village had not quite awoken either it seemed. I went to the back and started spinning, keeping the thread thick for warmer winter articles. The couple still bothered me. It was more than the speed of the courtship—that was not entirely unheard of, though usually the two were promised by their families and the courtship was a formality. Perhaps it was his "distraction" by some of the other ladies in town. I couldn't help but wonder how many, and how distracted. Holden had one of those as well, though to my knowledge he was still distracted. Perhaps that was part of it: why had this one suddenly chosen one girl and leapt to marriage? Truly his actions were just as strange as hers.

Some of my bother, I'm sure, was how he reveled in her attention. It is one thing to know I was bitter; it was entirely another thing to get over it. And that perhaps made it worse. But in the wake of seeing such a couple and how they fawned over each other, I yearned desperately to fawn over Thomas. He was every bit as handsome, without the baggage of having been "distracted." It wasn't fair. And so I worried about him as equally as I was mad at him.

The bell tinkled and I skidded the wheel to a stop. I had just turned to move to the front when I heard Tabitha call out: "Could you pull a few more bundles of flax, and right away, please? I'll be back there shortly."

"Yes, mistress," I replied. "We had a customer while you were away," I continued as I went up the ladder.

"Oh?"

I pulled myself into the attic. "Yes. Ordering a wedding dress. I took her measurements, and a shilling to start."

"Okay..." She seemed hesitant, and her voice now was coming from directly below.

"I'm sorry, I wasn't sure what else to do."

"No, it's fine. Who was it?"

I swallowed. "I'm afraid I didn't get their names. The whole event was...strange. I could probably describe them to you...?"

I stepped down the ladder. She was tucking something away in the closet, and shut the door quickly. "Go ahead," she prodded. I complied, and before getting halfway done with his description she nodded. "Maxime," she said. "Yes, well—wait, a wedding dress? For who?"

I began describing the girl, and again it took only a few words and I saw recognition dawn in her. And surprise. "Well he's tangled with a real one," she said. "I never would have thought it."

"Apparently the girl—what's her name? Julienne, she said she had been waiting for him."

Tabitha scoffed. "She's been waiting for anyone." Her lips pressed thin. "That was unfair. She is passing fair, but her father is known to be...difficult. I suspect whoever made it past him was the one she was waiting for. Maxime, though. I hate to admit I'm surprised. Well, we have a shilling and some measurements, so let's see where it takes us."

I gave her both, including the last I had remembered, as well as their request that it befit Julienne, and before the Mayor's wedding. Tabitha gave only the briefest smirk before pulling some bolts of cloth and setting to work.

"Oh, and I went to see Mr. Messick," she said as she threaded her needles. She eyed me. "You can go to see him right away. It seemed he was actually somewhat anxious to meet you."

I paused, my hands clasped. "Does that worry you?"

She shook her head. "Oh, no. He can be quite…capricious doesn't grasp it. Decisive?" She shrugged. "He settles quickly but firmly. I expect you'll be back before lunch, so don't worry about that. You'll need to take the cross road east. He's the house with the large shields on the door. Just ring the bell."

After throwing an extra cloak around my shoulders I stepped out into streets quickly growing busy. Shops were opening, caravans were preparing to depart, and there was still a general state of revelry going on by committed partiers. I wondered if they were somehow employed or directed by the mayor to be in a near-constant state of jubilation.

The air was crisp, and I could occasionally see my breath puffing out before me as I made my way toward the sun. I had begun to prefer mornings like this when I was in the convent, enjoying the invigorating chill. There was a thin but jagged line of white on the horizon, and I found myself thinking of Mahmoud. I hoped he was doing well on whatever business he attended.

A house caught my eye, and I wondered at it. Amid a collection of timber-frame homes and shops, it was built more like a castle of solid stone, mortared and smooth to prevent climbing. As I neared, I began to suspect whose house it was. When I saw the shields I rolled my eyes: Tabitha might have simply said it was the castle at the end of the street. It even had turrets, and ramparts. I expected a herald to be atop the gate.

Instead there was a bell-pull, which I pulled. The door was soon opened by a man of middle height in a flowing cloak of red, with a brown hand-felted cap covering a head of black hair. Dark eyes considered me a moment before brows lifted in question.

"Rae-Anna," I said. "To see Mr. Messick?" I wasn't sure why I formed it as a question, as though this might not be his residence.

"Ah!" he said, his eyes lighting up. "She said you might be prompt. I am Sir Jule." He leaned a little closer and lowered his voice. "A style of my master, not true knighthood. Perhaps at one time I might have, but..." He backed away and gestured me to enter. After he shut the door and led me down the hall, I saw his limp. No, he would never be a knight with that.

The hallway soon opened to a large room, and I nearly gasped. The walls were entirely obscured by tapestries, with some portraits hanging in front of those. No less than four suits of armor stood on pedestals in alcoves where arrow slits let in shafts of daylight. These shafts fell across bright carpeting and polished wood floors.

Sir Jule had paused and was watching me with a grin. "All have the same reaction when they see it," he said. "I am accustomed to waiting."

I smiled in return, following him again as he made for an oaken door to the right end of the room. As we passed one of the suits of armor, a strange chill wafted over me. I glanced sharply and thought perhaps I saw a set of eyes through the narrow slits of the helm. But when I looked closer they were gone—or was it only the sunlight? I peered through; perhaps there was a seam or crack at the back of the helmet. I shook my head and caught up to Sir Jule.

He opened this door, and it seemed another glow emanated from this room as well. "It is Rae-Anna, Thomas' friend," Sir Jule said. His tone was more clipped, more proper I suppose, but still with some familiarity.

I stepped through the door. One Mr. Messick, I assumed, sat in a large cushioned chair to the left of a roaring hearth, the chair's twin on the right. Tall windows let in armloads of sunlight that bounced off bright walls the color of buttercups. Yet another suit of armor stood in a corner, sword drawn with its point grounded between the suit's feet. Various potted plants dotted the walls on shelves, lending a grassy smell to the room. Other shelves held leather-bound books of various ages and colors. Under each of the shelves, and above the suit of armor, was the spiraling star symbol.

Mr. Messick and Sir Jule looked at me with identical smiles and glinting eyes. "Please," Mr. Messick said, his voice earthy and full of power. He waved a thick hand toward the chair beside him. "Sit with me."

Chapter 6

Mr. Messick was dressed warmly, but not opulently, and the colors were not so bright as the room. He was probably powerfully built when he was younger, and had only gone a little soft in age. I had no doubt he could move swiftly if he needed to. Sir Jule, now I looked closer at him, wore similar loose cloth that was not too loose—and also hid, I thought, powerful muscles underneath, despite his knee.

Tabitha said she trusted him—but she had the symbol in her shop with an un-verifiable excuse for it. And she had begun acting strangely, hiding things away, being gone from the shop at an odd time. Presumably to call on Mr. Messick, but what had she told him? Had they begun some conspiracy? What kind of threat did they think I was?

They both continued to stare at me. "Do you fear me?" Mr. Messick asked. His baritone was still gentle, but also still full of force.

"I am not from here," I said carefully. "And I've not had enough time to hear about most of the people of the village. Is it so strange to be cautious of someone I don't know?"

His hands clasped in front of him. "But it was you who asked for this audience."

"I asked for *an* audience, my lord." I wasn't sure why I gave him the honorific, but he didn't refute it either. "I wasn't expecting it so quickly, or in such...environs."

His smile seemed genuine, and calmed me a little. "Forgive me if that was part of my intent. Perhaps I should not have wasted it on you, but it is comfortable for me."

I gave a tight smile in return, then settled myself in the chair he had indicated earlier. It was firm, and felt little used. As I sat, Sir Jule bowed to me and left the room. Mr. Messick observed me, slightly askew in his chair. I wasn't sure what to do with my hands as I waited for him to speak. The silence stretched, until I cleared my throat lightly to break the silence.

"You requested the audience," he said again. I tried to read his eyes, but they were neither mirthful, angry, nor even curious.

"Yes," I said. I tried to keep from glancing at the symbols scattered around the room. I didn't expect to find them there, and now I was afraid to ask him about them directly. I found myself again wondering what kind of man he was, what his role was in the town. "It is comfortable for me to get to know a person, at least a little bit, before asking questions that might be"—I didn't want to say 'difficult'—"close. Personal, perhaps."

"I am the same," he said. "Tabitha tells me you have curious abilities."

I flushed. "I would not call them that."

"What would you call them?"

I fidgeted, not knowing his religion. My spirit chided me that it did not matter. "Not 'them'; 'he,'" I said firmly. "I have Our Father's

Sacred Fire in me, who works through me against The Liar and his followers. How he chooses to do that is up to him."

Mr. Messick lifted an eyebrow. "Putting out fires that catch almost instantly from embers?"

I shrugged, but looked pointedly at him. "They were fires from Abaddon," I said.

"And did your Sacred Fire warn you about me?"

I considered the sense inside. The flame was simply there. But I also remembered the strange chill walking past the suit of armor in the hall. "Perhaps that was only me," I admitted. "And I don't know who you are, aside from being Mr. Messick."

"And what do you want me to tell you?"

"Who you are, I guess."

He barked a laugh. "That may take some telling."

I shifted, feeling the symbols burning into the back of my head from their shelves. "Tabitha does not seem to know what to call you," I said instead. "You are not, nor were you the mayor. And yet, living as you do, with the power you seem to hold..."

"Power is a fascinating thing, my dear," he said. "The ease, sometimes, with which men confer it on one another. And yet at other times they waste themselves doing everything they can to keep it from someone. Some men use force, others use their intellect, still others use a fear that perhaps already exists and only stoke it higher. It can be a grubby thing, and yet it can move mountains."

"I thought faith moved mountains," I replied.

His eyes twinkled in the first fully-genuine smile I had seen him bestow. "And that, indeed, is a powerful faith. So your power, then, comes from this Sacred Fire?"

"As I said, it is not my power but a power that lives in me."

He raised a forefinger. "That is a very important distinction, isn't it? Curious how few would make it. But I do not think, then, that you requested this audience only to find out who I was?"

"Not entirely," I admitted. I took a deep breath. "I wondered what you knew about these symbols you have across your walls."

His eyes barely flickered. "Life," he said simply. "Perhaps one of the greatest powers there are."

"Below the one who gives it."

His smile was wan. "Of course."

"Where did it come from?"

"The symbol? Oh, I don't know. I came across it in one of my books and liked it. It catches the eye, doesn't it? So I came to mark everything into which I breathed life—those plants, the life which books give. Some of my suits of armor—did you notice? I assume they saved some valiant knight's life, and in thanks he marked it with that symbol."

I had not noticed, though I wondered now about the one in the outer room. "Do you know why the mayor's retinue wear that symbol on a medallion?"

He paused a moment with pursed lips. "I don't know if the mayor has heard of it, though it is of course possible. If so, perhaps he gave it to the paranymph—his closest attendant, as one who gives life to the wedding."

It did not explain why the evil men who appeared to me the first night would have it, or why the carpenter was so afraid of it, but I wasn't sure I wanted to open that discussion. It might be enough to get Henri talking.

"One last thing, if I may?" He gestured me to continue. "What does Thomas do for you? How did he come to work for you?"

"Errands," he replied. "Sir Jule, you may have noticed, does not get about as he once did. He is very useful to me, but there are things I need and I cannot be in two places at once."

"Did you send him to the shop yesternight?" I failed to keep fear and anger from my tone.

"I am finished with him by dinner," he said calmly. "Where he goes or with whom he meets after that is of no concern to me."

I did not like the bland way he said it—as though he knew Thomas had gotten himself into trouble but didn't care. "Please, my lord," I said. "He means a lot to me. If it is within your power to protect him, please do so."

His eyes glittered, and I worried I had pushed too hard by appealing to power. It was clear to me he had it—relished it, even, though subtly. I knew by so boldly suggesting he might not have that power it could anger him. But I wasn't sure what else to do.

Instead, he picked up a little bell and rang it. Shortly, Sir Jule returned and stood patiently smiling. "Thank you for meeting with me," I said as I stood. "And for being gracious to a young woman." I hoped that mollified him. His expression did not change as I left with Sir Jule.

Back through that impressive hall, I felt nothing from the suit of armor and no hint of glittering in the eye slits. The star symbol was lacking from that piece, though it was on the rest. Back on the street, I nodded to Sir Jule when he bowed, and the door was shut.

I spent the walk back to the shop lost in thought, sometimes barely dodging around someone I didn't notice as I mumbled my apologies. I had hoped to talk with Tabitha about my visit, and some of the things Mr. Messick had said, especially about the symbol.

But when I walked in a strange buzzing filled my head, a tension. I blinked owlishly in the mental sludge. Sounds came as though through thick walls. Another couple stood before Tabitha, their backs to me. No one took notice as the door shut behind me.

Tabitha's expression was the kind of resignation that came after a hard fight—I had seen it on the Sisters many times while I was there. I'm sure I wore it a lot too, back then.

The woman was in a pale blue frock and stood with her toes pointed inward just slightly, her hands clasped in front of her, her bonneted head bowed. The man stood rakishly before Tabitha, one hand sweeping his cloak back as he leaned against her counter. He towered over her naturally; it seemed he exuded dominance more than he wielded it.

Another owlish blink and I felt my gaze drawn to the symbol on the counter. But my eyes slid past it, then back again, like when I didn't want to meet Sister Judith's eyes but was told I must. I felt coldness in my stomach, a harsh winter's day inside nearly extinguishing the flame. I closed my eyes, wrapped the arms of my heart around that ember, coaxed it into life.

Fret not thyself because of evildoers.

The man laughed suddenly, and the walls were gone, the tension dripped away leaving only a faint hum behind. I remained still.

"Maxime!" he said again with a broad chuckle. "That cad. I'll speak to him. We both know how he is, don't we?" His eyes sparkled as he regarded Tabitha. I felt myself wanting to agree with him, even as little as I knew about Maxime.

"Even so, Claude, he was here first, and I've already begun work."

Claude's smile faded—or, seemed more forced. "Miss Tabitha, you are a lovely person," he said gently. "But surely you see that was *why* he was here so early in the morning. He knows Julienne will run like a jackrabbit as soon as her wits return, and he must be wed*locked* before that happens. You will be doing them both a service by making them think on things a little longer. The man has no control whatsoever!"

Tabitha's lips thinned a moment. "Yes, that is a failing of some, isn't it." I thought I saw Claude's jaw clench as his eyes narrowed. "I can do no work though, without specifications. So perhaps while my assistant measures your fiancée, we can discuss materials."

It seemed a marvelous plan on her part, and I nearly wanted to applaud her. Instead I stood smiling stupidly until I remembered *I* was the assistant, at whom everyone was suddenly looking. "Oh! Of course, this way please," I said to the girl, blushing furiously as I guided her toward the back. She gave me a tiny smile as she followed with mincing steps.

"Pick up your feet, darling," Claude said. My gaze darted to him as the girl made a little mewling noise. There were thunderclouds in those eyes of his, though the smile was still there too, like a sudden sunset peering out from underneath a storm. Though it was directed at her, it buffeted me as well.

We went into the back and I arranged the curtains. I gathered the implements again, thoughts troubled, as the girl prepared herself. I dared a glance at her as I began measuring. "What's your name?" I asked this time.

"Loana," she said briskly.

I blinked at her. "Loana," I repeated, writing it down. A thought brushed by—that I would likely never see these people again. I took their names because it would help Tabitha, and it made conversation easier. I wondered if, after they left, I would ever need their name again. My heart fluttered a moment at the impermanence of these relationships. And yet, it also meant I had the barest moments to perhaps speak Our Father's Kingdom to some of these. Far from making my itinerant lifestyle easier, the brevity of these meetings added a weight I suddenly knew I couldn't carry alone.

I returned to the young woman before me. "Your Claude is

a...handsome man," I said carefully.

She shrugged. "He'll do."

The measuring line slipped from my fingers. I apologized and measured again. "Are you excited for the wedding?"

She gave me a long-suffering look, but made no reply. I hurried on. I thought briefly of Thomas, of the idea of preparing to marry him. I was behind her then, and took a moment to calm an irrational heart. Especially since he might be in danger at this very moment. I wished I had seen him at Mr. Messick's, or had heard some news of him there. But I had forgotten to ask—hadn't I?

"Are we done, then?" Loana asked.

I startled. "I'm sorry, I had something on my mind." I continued a few measurements.

She sighed. "Look, it's not like he's a beast or something," she said. I hesitated, not sure why she was telling me, but I let her talk. "He likes to be in control—would you rather he be like Maxime? Or Paulo?" She bit the last name off, glancing at me chagrined as I came around the front again. "Please forget I said that last name." I shrugged; the name meant nothing to me yet. "Well, anyway, Claude thinks he can do anything—and I'm more than willing to let him."

"Anything?" I asked.

"Well, almost anything." The look she gave me was anything but timid. It was downright conniving, and I gaped. "Perhaps now you start to understand," she said slyly. "Oh, he thinks he's won—timidity can be a monumental conquest, if it's done properly. He spent a year trying to 'convince' me we could indeed be a good couple if"—her voice changed as she suddenly took on her assumed air—"I could just let him into my fluttering heart." She grinned almost evilly. "After that he's been positively...malleable." She paused. "I do trust you won't betray my confidence."

Her change in attitude bewildered my previous realization, and I could not even think where or how to insert Our Father's Kingdom into this woman's attitude. So I only smiled thinly. "Of course not. I'm only the assistant, it is not my job to interfere or advise couples in their marriages." I tucked away the measuring line and writing implements.

"Hmm. Very good." She dressed quickly, and I escorted her to the front again.

Tabitha was still staring icily at a grinning Claude when we came out. Immediately, Loana's head went down, and her toes pigeoned inward again as she minced toward him.

"Thank you, miss Tabitha," he said as they turned for the door. The little bell rang as they went out, and I felt the tension ebb and fade.

"I'm not sure that girl knows what she's getting into. Or has the power to stop it," Tabitha muttered.

I cocked an eyebrow. "Oh I don't know, it seems like she does." When she glanced at me I relayed the gist of our conversation in the back—to her ever-widening eyes. When I finished she shook her head.

"What a couple."

"They will be, I guess. There's a lot of weddings happening suddenly," I mused.

Tabitha shrugged. "With the mayor's upcoming so prominent on people's minds, I suppose it seems natural for everyone else to as well. I mean, if you're ever going to, why not do so alongside your town leader?"

"It seems contrived," I said.

"It is. But much of life is contrived, I guess. We wouldn't survive our days without some contriving."

"Speaking of, did you agree to his schedule?"

"Of course I did," she said. "But I predict a shortage of a certain cloth in the next few days, which I cannot help. Nor can he."

"Isn't that lying?"

She pursed her lips. "Call it contriving," she said with a sly grin. "If it makes you feel better, I gave him a range of time. The shortage will ensure I have the full extent of that range. How was your visit with Mr. Messick?"

As I followed her to the back, and picked up our work where we left off, I relayed the trip. "So I may have something to follow, with his explanation of the symbol. But I don't know if it'll be enough to crack open Henri's secrets."

"It also doesn't seem like something Henri would be afraid of." She shook her head. "I had hoped Mr. Messick would be more help than that. I'm honestly surprised..." She trailed off with another slight shake of her head. She trimmed a thread and backed away from the dress to inspect it a moment.

"Perhaps he still was," I said. "If he should have known more than what he seems to let on, then we know for certain the symbol means more than that—why would he hide it, otherwise? And Henri's reaction felt far more genuine than Mr. Messick's." We worked without talking for a time, the only noises either wafting in from the street or the clacking of the flax break. I wondered, suddenly, if Thomas could be "contrived" the way Loana did to Claude. It would have to be done carefully—he would notice too great and sudden a change. Perhaps I would work on my doe-eyes next time he came around. Just to see what he did.

I shook my head as Tabitha began humming again, that tune I could only vaguely remember. A childhood tune, I thought distractedly—or, something meant to attract and entertain children. And juggling: I could almost see the sun winking as colored balls and pins whirled through the air. Why did it strike me so? I remembered childhood laughter, the fascination of seeing those balls and pins spinning and flying. It had felt like magic, back then. There was the smell of grass, the evening sun, flaky and sugary pastries only to be had on that festival day. Had there been men on stilts, or was it only that I had been so small? And tumblers in bright clothing rolling and balancing. All of it magical for a child.

And there was a tent. It stood out in my mind because, unlike so much else, it was very drab. I felt the noise and colors drain away, the sun go behind a cloud, as I stared at the tent. A furtive shape ducked out, looking both ways before striding quickly away, hands buried in pockets. Another furtive shape entered. There was no sign to mark what it was. And yet I stood transfixed, sticky pastry in my hand, staring as all the magic and wonder faded away behind me.

The second figure emerged and ducked away like the first. There was no one else waiting. As I stared, the flap shifted and a woman stood in the opening. She crossed her arms and watched the second figure go, shaking her head with a bemused grin. Then she looked at me. I remember staring hard at her with the forthrightness of a child, and that tune jangled behind me, and my mother finally came and swept me away. As she carried me I continued to watch over her shoulder as the woman finally ducked back inside, and in the fading light of day I saw a symbol stitched into the door in thread nearly the same color as the door itself. A star in a swirled pattern.

The tune jangled again, and I started. It was the door bell. Tabitha rose, the hum dying on her lips as she went to the front. "Yes?" I heard her ask.

"From the mayor," the man's voice said. "He wishes your assistant to come to his manor on the morrow."

Chapter 7

Tabitha came back with a troubled look. "Did you hear that?" she asked.

I tried to keep the tremor from my voice. "You look like I should be worried."

She shook her head. "Not about the mayor himself—he's harmless. I never assumed he would call for you." She returned to her dress. "Well, this might be good, right? Perhaps he'll know something."

I tried to smile. "Right. Now that we know the symbol his paranymph carries is something to strike fear into Henri, make Mr. Messick lie, and…" I studied her. Unless she was very well preserved, she was not the same woman from my childhood. So how was it connected? "What is that song you hum every now and then?"

She glanced sharply at me, then relaxed. "Oh, that. I don't know, it makes me happy sometimes. Half the time I don't even know I'm doing it."

"Where did you hear it?"

She glanced away as she adjusted some fabric. "Hmm. Long ago, certainly. I think my papa used to sing it to me." Her features tightened suddenly, and she bent to her task.

"What happened to him?" I asked.

She was silent for a time, and I thought maybe she wouldn't answer. It was clearly something very close to her. I continued breaking flax. Finally she took a breath. "He was killed. Trampled. Supposedly it was an accident, but...well, the lord was known for his temper. And my papa was in the way."

She stopped talking again, and I let her. By her tone the story was darker and more complex than just that. "I think I heard it at a carnival that was passing through Holden," I said. "So it brings back some happy memories for me, too. I was only surprised we both had heard it, though I'd forgotten it until you hummed it."

She smiled at me. "I believe you're right," she said. "Now that you say it, I think I may have heard it at a carnival too. Maybe that's where my papa got it."

"Was there...was there a tent on the outskirts? Unmarked—well, no flashy banner like..." I trailed off as I caught Tabitha's suppressed laughter. "What is it?"

"Were there men furtively coming and going? But only one at a time?" she asked.

I nodded uncertainly, then gaped as the realization struck me. "You mean it was a—"

She nodded. "They're more common than you think. Usually they're set up a little further away, so I'm surprised you glimpsed it. But, in a way, it's perfect: the men get what they want, and the woman is gone. Usually no chance for unexpected responsibilities, at least on the part of the men."

"What happens to the women?"

"Oh, every now and then one will give birth, to be sure. It's hard to avoid that entirely, though there are sometimes potions you can buy from an apothecary. So she leaves off the circuit for a while. The child either joins the carnival, or they join a local monastery. Or convent," she added with an arched brow.

My smile was tight. "I was cursed, but I had parents in Holden."

"What did they think when you—?" She broke off when she saw my smile thin even more.

"I was cursed," I repeated. "They turned me out long before I went to the convent."

"Hmm." She sewed for a time, and I gathered the broken flax to take outside for scutching. As I made for the door, she said: "You know, as much as they may have rejected you for your curse, they might still want to know how you've turned out."

I paused in the open door. "If they refuse to help write the story, then they don't get to know the end," I said. I picked up the flail. "Now, if you don't mind, I'm going to go beat the Liar out of this flax."

I didn't blame her for bringing it up, so I was able to restrain my arm well enough to accomplish only the task at hand. And hers was generally good advice—just not specifically. Most of the feelings surrounding my parents included trying to survive alone in the streets of Holden. Others were of the severity of my mother—I could never do things exactly right—or the impotence of my father, who only sighed and walked away whenever my mother laid into me. The Sisters often said our view of Our Father was usually influenced by our view of our fathers. I believe mine was, just in the negative: if He were a true Father then He was supremely capable and did not stand idly by while His children suffered. It was *becoming* His child that was the difficult part.

That idea had changed in the Convent with the coming of the

Fire. Any difficulty in becoming a child of Our Father was in us, not in Him—in our own resistance to His call. Unlike my parents, He wanted to help us write our story, would be alongside us and give us strength to do what we could not.

I gathered up the threads of flax, now free of the smallest speck of woody debris. I inspected the fibers, tossed a few aside that had taken a little too much of my anger. Tossed aside, too, the thoughts of my parents. I was here, now, and had an assignment. And would go to see the Mayor tomorrow morning.

I brushed off my dress, tucked a wisp of hair away, caught my breath. I went back in, a smile ready for Tabitha. She was humming again, and quickly closed the closet door when I entered. "Thank you for caring," I said.

She looked askance at me for a moment, then brightened. "Oh, that. Well. I suppose I imagined...well, if I had ever been a mother..." She seemed startled by what she'd said, and smiled grimly. "But, I understand."

I returned the smile. "I don't even understand," I said gently. "And maybe we'll talk about it sometime and we can both try to understand. For now, what do I need to know before seeing the Mayor?"

"First," she said, smoothing her skirt, "you'll need something a little more appropriate to wear." She directed me to stand on the measuring stool. She arranged the curtains, then pulled out a woolen dress of a bright olive green. "It was mine, before my husband died," she explained as I stripped down to my shift. "I think it should just fit you."

The rest of the afternoon was spent in fitting it to me—it was a little tight, to start, which surprised me only because I usually swam in the clothes I received at the convent. Partially it was the style, she said, and she had never quite fit into it either. With a coy smile she remarked her husband had liked that part about it.

As she altered she told me a little of the Mayor—though young, he felt his power and was increasingly growing into it. He might over-look little foibles, but best not to press it. He preferred 'lordship'—a reach, but the people humored him and he hadn't yet begun to take it too seriously.

My greatest concern I didn't voice was that his entourage would be there. It felt very much like going in to the lions' den. Daniel had been forced into it because of his faith; I wasn't entirely sure why I was doing it—feared it was the result of my curiosity. I had been told for too long that Our Father did not reward something so idle as curiosity—only earnest and diligent seeking. So I worried I could not be sure of His protection.

"He may offer you wine," Tabitha was saying. "He's particularly proud of some of the local vintages. I would recommend accepting the first offer—it is rather good, actually. But don't worry about refusing a second. Make the first one last regardless."

I stared at her. "I haven't really had wine before," I admitted.

"Oh. Well then, you'll probably find it terribly revolting anyway."

"But I should still accept it?"

She stepped back and looked me up and down with a smile. "I think that should do nicely," she said. She cocked an eyebrow. "And wait until Thomas sees it."

I chewed my lip. "I didn't see him at Mr. Messick's today," I said as I took the dress off. "And the last time he was here..." I trailed off; we both knew.

"I'm sure he was just busy," Tabitha said, taking the dress from me. "Mr. Messick can be that way."

"He all but said he didn't care what happened to Thomas," I

replied. So I had asked—why didn't I remember, before? Was it Claude, or Loana, exerting some influence? Tabitha was gazing at me curiously, so I hurried to don my plainer dress. It was more comfortable, too. More...me. The other questions could wait.

"But he didn't say Thomas was no longer under his employ?"

I shrugged. "I guess not. But where is he, then?"

Tabitha folded the dress over her arm and smoothed it. "It's too early yet to worry."

"It feels like the perfect time," I muttered.

She smiled. "I know. But our town is not so dangerous as that."

As she turned to put the dress away, I grimaced to myself. Perhaps it had not been previously, but I would not be here if there was not some threat. And I was primping myself to walk perhaps directly into the middle of that threat, worried about whether I should drink wine or not.

I preparest a table before thee in the presence of thine enemies.

I reflexively looked at my hand. It had almost been more comforting when the fire was there. At least, that's what I told myself then. It was false; and yet, once I had accepted it for what it was, there was a deal of comfort to be had there. Comfort in the physical presence of something.

But if we hope for that we see not, then do we with patience wait for it.

My, but he was suddenly talkative. I wondered if he had any wisdom concerning Thomas?

But there was nothing. I bit my lip. Tabitha turned and, seeing it, mistook the expression. "I'll ask around if I can," she said. "But for now, I've got dresses to make. Would you mind spinning me a little more thread? I suspect we have not seen the last couple looking to wed during the festival weeks."

I forced on a smile and set to work, passing the rest of the day swiftly.

The next morning Tabitha showed me where I could accomplish something of a bath, and set to braiding my hair in a complicated way that felt far too extravagant for my head. When she'd finished, I had to admit, however odd it felt, it looked good on me when set with the dress. I felt a pang wishing Thomas *could* see me like this—perhaps it might soften him toward me.

But that was not today's task. It needed to soften the mayor toward me. I hoped, in his presence, the strange men of his entourage would be unable to threaten me. Or, even better, they wouldn't be there. But the Fire had said the table was set in their presence, for I did not yet consider the mayor an enemy.

The little bell rang, and the messenger from yesterday entered. "I need to stay here anyway," Tabitha said as I looked imploringly at her. "There is much to do, and...well, as I said, I don't think we've seen our last customer."

The messenger looked me up and down, and seemed to approve without being lascivious. He walked ahead, bringing us quickly to the north end of town where the mayor's house was nestled among a small grove of trees. The arborvitaes were well kept and presented a small screen, just enough to set the manor slightly apart without separating it entirely from the rest of the village.

The manor itself was Roman, lacking only the defensive wall. Guards were posted in a small outbuilding by the road, and nodded to the messenger as we walked by. I gave the faintest smile as they turned back to the man who appeared to me to be a merchant presenting his request for trade.

The displays of celebration in town were multiplied here by several. As we neared the door I spied an arbor set in a broad field, festooned with white blossoms, lace, and wicker. I frowned; had he determined not to wed in the cathedral?

But then we were passing inside. There was a low bustle—the wedding itself was not for some time yet, I thought, and preparations would not reach a pitch just yet—and we made our way into the interior. We quickly arrived at the dinner hall. I quirked an eyebrow, then took a breath to smooth my features. I was his guest.

The messenger announced me and I stepped inside. There was a scattering of people at the tables, most of whom had no obvious trades. Of those who did, the blacksmith startled me the most as he sat, still in leather apron, eating with a slightly hunted look. As I glanced around again I noticed most of the people there were not completely at ease.

"Rae-Anna!" the mayor called cheerfully enough. I looked to the head, seeing him sitting with four of his entourage—only the leader was missing. And there was an empty chair right next to the mayor, to which he gestured with a smile.

I swallowed; I had not expected the meeting to be in public, and for me to be seated so near him. His fiancée was nowhere to be seen. Was that why it was public, then? And these people called against their wishes?

I curtsied as best I could and made my way to the head of the table. A servant slid the chair out for me, tucking it back in as I sat. Servers quickly appeared and loaded my plate with thinly sliced meats, two kinds of cheese, and warm bread drenched with a creamy soup.

"I know it is early, but would you have some wine?" he asked.

"That would be very generous, thank you," I replied, trying to sound as calm as I could. I hoped, like Saint Timothy, it might settle my stomach.

Another servant poured the apple-clear wine into a silver goblet. I scented it as I raised it to my lips, surprised by a mix of sweet fruit and fermented rot. Taking the smallest sip I could, it shocked me how dry the liquid felt as it passed over my tongue. I stared at the wine as I set the goblet down.

"Does it suit you?" the mayor asked.

I glanced at him. It still surprised me how young he was—or, seemed. Now I was closer it was easier to see the wrinkles around his eyes that had been filled in with paste and powder. "I must confess, lordship, it is the first I've tasted wine," I said. "It is...unique."

He smiled broadly but did not laugh. "And now I've spoiled you by giving you the best first. I'm afraid every wine after this will only disappoint you."

I smiled demurely, refraining from telling him I might never have it again. And yet, as I ate, I found myself returning to that goblet frequently. It grew on me, my tongue beginning to yearn for the taste, the feeling of it passing over and down my throat. Tabitha's warning to deny a second glass came and went.

I began to feel full, and sat back from the plate. I swept my gaze once more over the other dining guests, their furtive glances striking me only dully. The mayor was correct: this seemed an exceptional wine.

"Mr. Messick tells me you show some interest in an ancient symbol," the mayor said close by.

I turned to him and blinked. "It's a unique, um, thing," I said, and giggled. "I'm sorry, my speech seems mixed now."

He smiled warmly. "It happens. And you notice the unique, do you?"

"Of course," I said. "It also seems unique to me that such a unique symbol is suddenly cropping up everywhere." Almost against my will, my hand reached for the goblet again and I took another sip.

"It has some history in this town," he said. "Coming, I've been told, from across the northern sea."

"Across—all the way from there?" I asked, impressed. Something about that struck me strange, but I couldn't organize my thoughts. "And what did it mean, all the way up there?"

"Are you familiar with the story of Cillian and Siobhan?"

I shook my head.

"Ah. A sad story, in the end. They were two lovers who could never quite come together. First one thing then another tore them apart—family demands, then misunderstanding, then war, and ultimately death. In the story, it was determined the stars simply never aligned—thus the whirling pattern as the lives of the lovers danced together, then apart."

"Mr. Messick said the symbol indicated life," I said, surprised the thought came to me so clearly.

The mayor's eyes flicked to the goblet and back. "To him, perhaps it does—so much of life is chasing something that may never be found. To others—like me—it symbolizes love: the relentless pursuit of the most divine experience here on earth."

Now it was on my mind again, I picked up the goblet and raised it to my lips. But as I did I looked up, seeing in the mayor's glance a predatory gleam. I looked past him to where two of his attendants sat, their eyes also peculiarly fixed on me. Two waves of emotions battered against me—anger that they seemed to manipulate me into drinking more wine than I had intended, and a loathing for myself that I had allowed them. I suddenly felt as though I had no control, had never had control. That I was and should be a leaf before their wind, to blow wherever they pleased.

I felt eyes pricking me from behind as well, and the room whirled as I turned to look. Those two loomed over me like massive shadows, their eyes like Cillian and Siobhan's stars glinting at me. I desired nothing more than that sweet wine, the pricking and then dulling of my senses of it. It seemed right, even if just for the moment, to live as I saw fit. I nearly gulped the rest down right then.

But then a door boomed and their gazes broke from me. The thoughts and emotions fled instantly, sucking me dry and empty, my mind spinning in a void.

"Paulo!" a woman's voice shouted. She was not devoid of emotion, not by a long shot. I blinked blearily at her. She was an older woman, and stood nearly vibrating at the entrance to the hall.

"Mother, I asked not to be disturbed this morning," the mayor said wearily.

"I can imagine," she replied, still huffing. "Fortunately one of your servants has more sense than you do, and told me what you were attempting."

I tried to glance between the two, but felt my head spinning. I suddenly couldn't remember how many goblets I'd had. And where I knew the name "Paulo" from—it had been a negative comparison, hadn't it?

"I was attempting, mother, to explain to this young woman a bit of Aurden's history."

She set her jaw stubbornly. The other guests suddenly seemed very interested in their food. She said something quietly to the manservant beside her. His eyes flicked to me, then the mayor, then back down. He strode quickly to the head, standing behind me with his hands on my chair.

I swallowed and scooted back. When I stood shakily, the servant's hand was on my arm to steady me.

"Forgive me," I said over a thick tongue, "if I do not show you proper deference, your lordship, and skip the curtsy." I swallowed. "I'm not sure I would rise again."

As I left with the servant, I spared a glance for the woman, but her eyes only glared fury at her son. The passage out through the halls went by in a blur, and before I knew it I was standing outside the manor, alone.

With jellied knees I slowly made my way back to the shop.

Chapter 8

Tabitha startled when I entered the shop. She ran over as I nearly collapsed. "What happened?" she demanded, supporting me in strong arms toward the back.

Every movement hurt by now. "I don't think I can make it up the ladder," I said, or at least I tried. Most of the words came out. More importantly none of my food came out. I considered that a great victory in the moment.

She changed directions, taking me to her room instead. "I told you to only take one cup," she said. To my dulled senses, I couldn't tell if she was angry, how much, or with whom. I think I began to cry. "Oh, hush now, it's my fault too. I should have advised you better when you told me you'd never had any before."

We stumbled into her room—she was strong but we all have our limits, and my legs had all but given out—and she managed, somehow, to prop me up enough to pull the covers back on her pallet. The room pitched and whirled as she lay me down.

"I think there was something else in it," I said, closing my eyes.

"His mother came in near the end of the meal and berated him for what she thought he intended."

Tabitha was silent; when I squinted at her, she seemed troubled. She caught my eye and shook her head. "I'm sorry for that," she said. "I would never have thought—was that why he wanted you there, then?"

I shook my head, then clapped a hand to it as though that might stop the spinning. "I don't think so. He did speak of the symbol. He told me a story about Cillian and Siobhan?" Tabitha seemed unfamiliar. "Apparently the symbol, to the mayor, means 'love' not 'life.' Though he believes the two are interchangeable—or nearly."

"I suppose that makes sense." She clicked her tongue. "What doesn't make sense is the mayor doing something like this!" Now it seemed very clear who she was angry with. "I can assure you, Rae-Anna, he has never been like this before. And I never would have sent you there—or told you to drink his wine—if I knew he was like that. What could possess him?"

Even in my addled state I had an idea. When Loana had likened a "Paulo" to Maxime, the name meant nothing. Now I could only imagine she knew the mayor to be as distracted by young women as Maxime had been. But in that moment I wanted to simply sleep. The door bell tinkled, and my eyes fluttered closed. I think I fell asleep in the midst of Tabitha excusing herself.

When I awoke, the room was still empty. I blinked a few times, afraid to move my head and find everything still swirling. But my thoughts seemed clearer to me. I turned and looked aside, seeing a simple clay cup beside the pallet. I levered myself up on my elbows, and took a drink from it—only clear, cold water. There was also a crust of bread. I took a few more drinks to wet my parched mouth before eating it.

I slid into a sitting position. Aside from being hungry, I felt okay. Ashamed, perhaps, and worried. I wondered how many had seen me staggering through town like a drunk. Most of them would not have necessarily known I had been to the mayor's first, especially since I didn't have the escort that time. I had to smirk at the intelligence of it: wouldn't want to discredit him right before his wedding.

Then why do any of it? The answer, quite simply, would be to discredit me. Any public statement I made after this could be attributed to the ravings of a drunkard, perhaps even of a spurned whore. Why else would I have been thrown out unattended?

Before I could sort through any of that, I needed food. I rose, realized I was still in the beautiful dress Tabitha had given me, and exited her room into the front of the shop. There was no one inside, and the daylight coming through the windows seemed to be fading. So I had slept through most of the day.

I made my way to the back, peering in. Tabitha was working on another of the dresses, humming her song. I stepped in, accidentally startling her. She looked me up and down as I stood, still in my shame. "I'm sorry," I said.

She took a deep breath. "Thomas was here," she said.

My eyes jumped to hers. When I saw her face, my heart slowed. "What…what happened?"

"I'm afraid rumors have started," she replied. "The story coming from the manor does not quite align with yours."

I chewed my lip. "I wondered if they would not," I said. "Who supposedly started the rumors?"

She took a breath. "Well, one of the servants, the blacksmith, the cobbler, two farmers, a shepherd, and three merchants. And, I think, the mayor's mother."

"And I got myself drunk and tried to entice the mayor away from his fiancée?"

She looked sharply at me. "Apparently you weren't concerned with the fiancée either way, as long as you got what you wanted." I snorted. "Did you overhear him, then?" she asked. "Or is that actually what happened?"

"When I left, his mother seemed furious with him, not me," I said.

"Yes, apparently she actually meant that for you—she meant to say a servant told her what *you* intended."

I looked at her askance. "Fascinating that they included such a detail in their 'rumors'," I said drily.

She considered that for a moment. "It is, isn't it."

Fear settled deep into my gut. "What did you tell Thomas?"

She wiped her hands down her lap. "I said you were safe, that it seemed a very strange story, that you had never indicated you would attempt such a thing...that he perhaps knew you better than I did."

I wondered. And worried; I didn't know what he thought of me anymore. "Did he seem...strange at all?"

She shook her head. "Just concerned. Maybe a little angry."

"Wonderful." I took a deep breath and rubbed my hands down my face. "I thought the worst would be that I could no longer speak publicly against the mayor's entourage, not that my traveling companion might not want anything to do with me anymore."

She rose, then, and came and put her hands on my shoulders. "First, I don't think Thomas will give up on you so easily. Second, you are otherwise unharmed, and at least you know Thomas is alive. And thirdly, I have decided not to throw you out." She gave me a small smile.

I tried to enjoy the jest, but I could also tell there was some truth in her joke; until I had convinced her otherwise, she had been set to turn me out. The edge I walked on frightened me—and that the mayor had acted so maliciously and near-perfectly against me. I would never had expected it of the one who had appeared in the shop those few days ago.

"Thomas alive and un-possessed are both good things," I managed. "And thank you for believing me."

"You are not the first woman to have false accusations leveled at her to discredit her," she said.

I chuckled. "Nor is it the first time it's happened to me, now you mention it."

She squeezed my shoulder and turned back to her dress. "What will you do now?" she asked, settling herself again.

"Eat?" I said.

Her eyes danced. "I saved you some," she said, gesturing to the table. "The advantage of cold lunches," she continued as I sat. "They are no worse for being left out a little longer."

It was mostly fruit and vegetables. I assumed I had already eaten the bread. And more water, which agreed with me the most. I chewed the victuals as I chewed over my thoughts. "There's more here that still doesn't fit," I mused as my plate neared empty. "Because neither of the stories explain why Henri was so terrified. And the story the mayor told—Cillian and Siobhan...Those names sound—"

"From the Celts," Tabitha said, nodding. "Do you think it originated there?"

Celts. Druids. It seemed forever ago I had the vision of the druid circles and dancers whirling. I wondered suddenly if they danced a star-pattern. I couldn't remember. "Perhaps. Which ties it strangely to what happened near Holden," I said.

"Does it all come from there, then?"

I considered. "I don't like to think so. It all comes from the Liar, first and foremost." And the fact that the druidic dancers seemed just as constrained as I had been, not necessarily evil in themselves—only, perhaps, more opened to its influences, as I was before I accepted the Sacred Fire. And besides that, the chant the skeletons had sung was not Gaelic. I didn't feel the need to elaborate on that for her. "But part of me wonders if it has more history with Aurden than anything else. That was what the mayor said when his mother came in, that he'd been explaining a bit of Aurden's history."

"Hm. Interesting. Perhaps it held some power in earlier days?"

I shrugged, and chewed through the last radish. "I think it may have. And perhaps one more learned in it would interpret the room at Mr. Messick's very differently."

"Do you think Henri, then—?" She cut off as the door bell rang. With a mild *tsk* she rose and went to the front.

I considered the question she had begun. Henri was definitely the next step. He knew far more of it—or, at least, far more of the darkness surrounding it—than anyone else was letting on. It struck me that I would have thought little of the symbol if it had not been carried by the demonic men that first night. I would likely not have even mentioned it to Henri, and certainly wouldn't be pursuing it further now. I wondered why they showed themselves so early: had they seen what they thought would be a frightened little girl? Someone they could easily overpower? I wondered too how surprised they were that I was far stronger than they thought, and I had to smile.

"Rae-Anna?" Tabitha called. I turned as she brought back another young woman. "Measurements please?"

We traded wide-eyed glances and I quickly turned with a smile to the young woman. "Of course! What a happy day," I said. She smiled demurely, and I led her to the pedestal as Tabitha returned to the front.

"What is your name?" I asked as I retrieved all-too-familiar implements.

"Chloé," she said quietly.

"Beautiful," I said with a smile to reassure her. "I'll need your dress off, though, to measure you properly. You can keep your shift on," I added quickly as her eyes widened.

"He won't see?" she asked.

I shook my head firmly. "Tabitha keeps him up front where he cannot see in. It's just us."

She mouthed a silent "okay" and began, stiffly, to disrobe. I hoped she wouldn't mind the occasional touch where I would hold the measuring line. Perhaps I could get her to help me. I took her dress from her and folded it over the chair, then handed her one end of the line and told her where to hold it.

"Have you been together long?" I asked. My mind couldn't help but dart back to some of the previous couples we had come through.

She nodded, but offered no more. I looked at her. "Chloé, this goes much better and easier if we trust one another," I said quietly. "You don't have to be afraid of me, or of anything really, while you're back here. And sometimes talking helps take your mind off your fears."

She shrugged and fumbled the line, dropping it to the floor. I only smiled and retrieved it, handing it back and telling her where to hold it next.

"He's courted me maybe four years," she said.

I raised my eyebrows appreciatively. "Good for him—and you," I said.

She flashed a grin. "Papa certainly approved. Mam...well..."

"You'll always be your mother's daughter," I said.

She sniffed. I wrote down the measurements. "She's not my actual mam," she said. Her voice grew strong for a moment, but then faded again as she smiled bitterly. "She...she expects much from me."

I drew a breath, waiting to reply until I had gotten the next measurement. "It can be very difficult to live up to expectations, sometimes. And harder for some expectations than others."

"Not Louis," she said. "He appreciates me exactly as I am."

"He is kind to you?" I asked.

"Kind!" she said, sounding hurt. "He lays no burden on me, and does everything to remove any burden I do carry."

I felt a faint stitch, thinking of some of the things I had endured in the convent. "Chloé," I began, thinking to remind her of how the oak grew strong—but I thought of Thomas, and our fight, and how I wished he hadn't suddenly started being harsh with me. I smiled. "It sounds wonderful—he sounds like a wonderful man, indeed. I'm so happy for you."

Her smile this time was genuine, and comfortable. I finished the measurements, helped her dress, and led her back to the front. Perhaps my lot in life was suffering and hardship, but I would begrudge no one a life unlike mine.

Tabitha finished up, thanked them, and they left. As soon as the door shut she turned to me looking aghast. "We cannot take many more of these," she said, and we laughed. Truly it would do nothing more than aid her business, but I could tell she had not had this many customers in a long time.

I had secretly determined to stay with her that evening, prepare as much raw material as I could. But after dinner, as she set herself before one of the dresses, she looked at me most severely. "You don't even think about carding or spinning tonight," she said. "I want you to go see Henri, to thank him again for his splendid work on our back door. And anything else you want to talk to him about."

I drew a breath to argue, but her brow arched, and I said only "thank you," and smiled. Part of me, I think, was afraid of what Henri would say, of what I might uncover if he did tell me the truth. And yet I knew it needed to be done.

"Take an extra cloak," she said, gesturing to the closet. "Or, let me get it for you," she said suddenly, all but leaping up. "It is getting rather cold, these nights," she said as she went inside. "And darker earlier. Henri is not far off the main road though," she continued as she came back out, cloak in hand. "Go like you're going to Mr. Messick's, but turn left at the third street. His will be the fourth house—he has a carved boar's head above his door." She shook her head as though she didn't know why he chose that as his marker. I couldn't imagine, either. She handed me the cloak, and I thanked her again.

It was indeed already dark outside, though the main roads were lit well enough by moonlight and the occasional lamp hanging by shop's doors. I counted the roads as I passed, turning at the third one.

It was a narrow lane, and the roofs overhung, blotting out the sky. The alley grew inky black, and I blinked to try to adjust my eyes. Another step, another blink, and five cloaked men were suddenly in front of me. Before I could scream the leader's hand was over my mouth, and his maggot-white face loomed near mine.

"Where isss your god?" he sneered.

Terrified I reached inside, but could not feel the flame over the iciness that gripped my stomach. My fingers pried at his, but could not loose them. As I gasped through my nose the stench of death pervaded me. It felt as if his fingers were inside my head, poking around, sliding slimily through my thoughts as though he sought a particular one. I shuddered, convulsed. I tried to wish for the blood to appear on my hands as it had the first time, but he seemed to grasp that thought and it shriveled. I thought of Thomas and his sword—

There was a sharp yank and suddenly I couldn't move. I felt the thought like a string pull through me as his hand withdrew. His sneer widened into a malevolent grin. "Thank you," he said. I could only gape at him; I still had no control over my body. He turned away, and one of the others stepped forward. Where the leader was narrow of face and nose, this one was round with a slight hook as his nose slanted toward his mouth. My body shivered as he stared at me with eyes that seemed to consume my vision. Suddenly his mouth opened wide—wider than any human mouth could go as he drew a whistling breath that never filled his lungs. The wind whipped down the alley, past me, into the cavern of his mouth. The whistling grew into a shriek. It seemed to me as if he was drawing the entire alley into himself. The walls stretched and pulled toward him; the stars above began to streak toward him. My own skin flaked off and rushed toward his mouth. The entirety of my reality seemed as though it were painted on a canvas and then slowly pulled through a funnel into impossible darkness.

Then everything was black. The shrieking died away and there was only a vacant hum in my ears. I could see nothing, hear nothing, and I felt myself falling backward though I never hit the ground. Only fell, and fell, until I was senseless.

Chapter 9

This next part of my story will only make sense if I tell it as I experienced it, not as I understand things now.

As awareness finally came back, I was falling again, as though I hadn't stopped. Then, slowly, I began to feel fire—not the Sacred Flame of Our Father, but as though I were in a furnace. And more than simply heat; I could feel each tongue of flame wavering back and forth over my skin. And though it hurt, I did not scream. I felt, after a time, that I should. But I could no more draw a breath or use my voice than I could move my arms or legs.

Finally, by degrees, I felt what seemed to be the touch of cold water, starting with my head and slowly working its way to my feet. How long this took I cannot say, but it was incremental. By the time it had reached my toes, the heat had begun at the top of my head again. And again the cool water began behind it.

The hum in my ears began to fade. It had never been audible, more of just a vibration, and as that diminished sounds came to me. Voices, though I could make out no language spoken. Just the occasional punctuation, perhaps as individual syllables rose above the hum. In those brief sounds there was a familiarity in the tone. But at the time, between the heat, the coolness, the hum, the inability to move or to make myself hear better, I knew mostly despair and so I did not even try to understand.

I wished for complete unconsciousness again, but it wouldn't come. The sensation of falling made me nauseous. I never grew accustomed to it. Then, finally, one word broke through, complete but unfamiliar:

"Rayanna?"

The humming seemed nearly to cease. I felt the word drawing me. My descent slowed, then I hovered in the chasm. I knew if I struggled I would fall again, but if I stayed still...

I slowly began to rise. It seemed to me as though I would have to rise just as far as I fell. I worried, suddenly, that I would have to rise through all that fire and water again. But now I was powerless. Quite apart from myself I flew up and up, faster and faster till I thought I should break through the heavens themselves.

And then I stopped. I thought I should lurch, or that I should have hit something, but I didn't. I realized I could hear. I could sense space around me, and felt a rough blanket covering me. A cool, wet rag was on my forehead. I could not open my eyes, but I could squeeze them just a little tighter shut, and then relax.

"Rae-Anna," the voice whispered. I vaguely felt the importance of this word, knew it was a name. *My name?* I thought so only logically at first. I squeezed my eyes shut again. My jaw loosened only enough to move a little. And, like thunder in my ears after so much silence, I made a croak.

"Praise Our Father," the voice said. The rag was lifted; I heard a splash, then drops falling into a bucket, and the rag came back refreshed. It was a woman's voice that had spoken, older than me I thought. But not old.

My tongue loosened. "Tab'tha?" I managed just above a whisper.

"Yes, Rae-Anna, I'm here. Oh, child. I have not prayed for one since..." She broke off, and as I tried to finish her sentence I fell asleep.

I awoke again, and my eyes opened. The room was dark except for some moonlight coming through a window somewhere. My body ached in every joint, and all my skin felt raw. I was terrified. I could not remember what happened, where I was, or how I got there. None of the night's events were with me, at that time. It was as if I had been born fully formed, with only the names Rae-Anna and Tabitha in my mind. And sometimes, lying in the dark, I could not remember if either of them were mine.

And there was something else, amid the ache and rawness and emptiness: a flame, as though there were a candle where I could not see, illuminating not so much with a physical light as it was a sense of understanding. I did not possess that understanding, but I was assured it would come. I slept again.

I awoke to daylight. I heard humming again, this time quite natural. It was a tune that brought me a sort of menacing joy—a childhood memory tainted by evil. As I had when I was in the chasm, I did not reach for it, but merely lay and listened.

The humming ceased, and I heard footsteps. A shadow fell across me, and the footsteps suddenly hurried. The woman—the owner of the voice I had heard, by her look—knelt beside me. "Rae-Anna?"

"Is that one mine?" I asked.

Her brow furrowed. "What one?"

"The name," I said. "I couldn't remember if it was Rae-Anna or Tabitha."

She laid a cool hand on my forehead. "Yes, your name is Rae-Anna. Mine is Tabitha."

"Oh. That's a nice name."

A grin quirked her lips. "Which one?"

I drew a deep breath, painful near the end. "Oh, both of them." I coughed once, iron bands squeezing my chest. "What happened?"

"I was hoping you could tell me," she said. "You don't remember anything?" I only looked at her and blinked. "Right. Your name. Well, what I know is this: Henri heard a noise like a great wind and when he came out, he found you in the alley, alone, and—" She stopped suddenly, her lip quivering.

"Henri is the carpenter," I said slowly. "I went to see him. But I didn't actually make it to see him. Why did I go to see him?"

"Well, because…" She rubbed her jaw. "I wanted you to take him something. For fixing our door." She looked away suddenly, picked at a fold in her dress.

"Am I your daughter?" I asked.

Her eyes darted to mine, but then she smiled softly. "In The Beloved," she responded.

At the name, more pieces fell into place. The convent, the Fire, the call of my journey though I couldn't recall the journey itself. Aurden. "I've been helping you make clothing—dresses," I said. "Wedding dresses, lately. A lot of them." It bothered me, how many wedding dresses she was making.

She laughed. "Yes, indeed. All the eligible ladies in Aurden are getting married it seems, to men whether they're eligible or not." She rubbed her jaw again and shrugged. She caught the horrified look on my face and laid a hand on my shoulder. "Oh they're not already married, any of them. Their prospects are just not necessarily what they should be to take a wife."

"Oh. Well I'm sure they'll find a way, if they really love each other."

Her face took on an even more mollifying look. "Of course they will. I shouldn't have spoken. I meant no harm by it. And I'm sure you and Thomas will find your way, as well."

The name struck me like a fat drop of rain, but beaded and ran off. "Who?"

"Thomas? The young man you came here with?"

I blinked. "I came here with someone? What was their name?"

She stared a moment. "I'm sorry. Maybe you should rest a little more. Eat this," she said, suddenly pointing beside me. I looked and saw a plate of bread and cheese and a sliced apple, and my stomach rumbled. "And then sleep, if you can."

I thought surely I could not. But as soon as the plate was empty and the cup drained I dutifully laid down.

I woke once, to moonlight again, then slept. I dreamed that time, walking empty streets while a walking staff tapped behind me and that childhood tune echoed from somewhere. Ahead of me a fire flickered, always around a bend so I only saw the light it cast. I began to run to it. It never seemed to move, but was always just ahead. In each alleyway I passed there was a strange knight in armor, sword grounded between his feet, sometimes near the road I was on, sometimes far distant and obscured by shadows. Occasionally I felt I could see his eyes; other times it was a hollow shell. I tried to stop, once, to look more closely. But my feet carried on without me and I again pursued the light. Finally I turned, and the street ended in sunrise.

I woke to the twittering of birds and early light against the wall. I got up and made my way through the shop and out the back door to the privy. It was cold, and frost clung to the grass. When I came back in, I found Tabitha glancing wildly about her room with a surprised look on her face that softened when she saw me. "There you are. I wasn't sure you would be up already," she said, stepping toward me. "Are you well-rested?"

I nodded. "I think so. I'm hungry, but otherwise..."

She nodded, but seemed afraid to look at my face. "Your speech is better," she said. "And you look...you look good. You look well. Hale, again."

I studied her. "I've never looked hale in my life," I said with a grin. I could feel my skin stretch, and my lips didn't grin quite right. Still unused to moving, I thought. I lifted my hands to rub some life into my face.

"Don't—!" Tabitha's hand was raised, but went to her mouth as I touched my cheek.

It burned. My fingers recoiled, then gingerly explored a cheek I was unfamiliar with—pocked and lined, and sensitive. Like when you've torn the skin off a blister. I sucked in a breath. I couldn't take my hands away even though they stung. "What happened to me?" I whispered.

Tabitha's eyes brimmed. "We don't know," she said. "I didn't even know if you would live, when Henri brought you here. Your face was completely raw as though all the skin had been torn from it."

I remembered the feverish sense of heat and cold, all that time falling through the dark. "Just my face?" I asked.

"There were cuts and scrapes other places, but not as bad. And those seemed to have healed. I was a little surprised at that. I rarely left your side, but any time I came back they were visibly better."

I finally let my hands drop. "But not my face."

"Rae-Anna, I thought you would die. Perhaps the skin has not fully healed yet, but it is no less miraculous."

I took a shaky breath. I couldn't remember any of it, and so I had to trust her. Perhaps it had been that bad. It didn't make the scars any less painful, though. And, for some reason, how I looked was important to me—not generally, but specifically. As though there were a particular person I thought I needed to be beautiful for. It seems impossible now, but at that time I couldn't remember who.

"Let's eat a little something and talk," she said. "I of course don't expect you to work today—"

"No, I think I should," I said. "I feel well enough. And you have these dresses to make—do you still have dresses to make?"

"Oh yes," she said. "Two are ready. Two more to go, so far."

I tried to furrow my brow, but that hurt too. "How long was I asleep?" I asked.

"Just a few days," she said. "None of the weddings have taken place yet."

We sat and ate, made light conversation. As we talked, little details fell into place until I thought I had a good grasp of my life—all except my supposed traveling companion, and the night I received my injuries. Had I been attacked? And by whom? Hopefully not my companion. I only remembered turning the corner to go to Henri's. But I couldn't remember for myself why I had gone, and so I accepted Tabitha's excuse.

Eventually, when I could no longer take her avoidance of my face, I got up and began to work. I needed the distraction, and a sense of solitude, or at least of being apart. I could adjust my chair and face away from her as I spun thread, and just think. Though many of the memories were there, most of the senses were not. I could not recall how I *felt* during the events at the convent, or at any of the meetings I recalled having in Aurden. And the information there too was disjointed: why did I care about the plants and suits of armor at Mr. Messick's? What was the glittering there that I remembered only vaguely? Why did I need to discuss Aurden's history with the mayor, and why had I tried to proposition him? I felt a brief flicker of shame at that, but it was quickly eaten by the flame.

Again, those memories slid by. That Fire had protected me in the convent—physically, but also mentally and emotionally. I remembered words coming to me at various but frequent times, back then. Yet somehow, since coming to Aurden, it had been strangely silent. And it had not kept me safe from whatever happened outside Henri's. *Where were you then? Why didn't you help me?*

And these words shall be in thine heart: And thou shalt talk of them when thou sittest in thine house, and when thou walkest by the way, and when thou liest down, and when thou risest up.

My fingers slipped, and I hurriedly caught the wheel before the too-thick thread was caught up in the spool. I backed it away, restarted, blinked away a tear so I could see what I was doing.

For if these things be in you, and abound, they make you that ye shall neither be barren nor unfruitful...

I sniffled, but kept on.

...but he that lacketh these things is blind, and cannot see afar off, and hath forgotten that he was purged from his old sins.

I stopped the wheel again and bowed my head—whispering, I think, the first prayer I uttered since arriving in Aurden. Oh there had been cursory graces, and one offered in desperate haste. But I had not contemplated The Beloved or even really the Sacred Fire since...I cocked my head. I'd had a fight—an argument with someone. Someone who mattered a great deal to me. Who had it been? Not Tabitha. Was it who I had traveled with? I only remembered Mahmoud, and he was not that precious to me...

But seek ye first the kingdom of God, and his righteousness...

I shook my head. How had I become so easily distracted? Starving myself of His presence, I had come to rely on my own power again. *Power. Life. Love.* Those were important somehow. I took another deep breath. And so when I went to Henri's, whoever attacked me had only to contend with me. I had abandoned The Fire, The Beloved, and my attackers fought only against flesh and blood.

I felt myself caving inward, threatening to collapse as tears coursed down my face. How utterly foolish I had been! How inexplicably stupid! As though our great and majestic Father were a winter's cloak only to be pulled out after our own warmth fell short for our needs, and not a dear companion to spend our every waking moment with. *Henceforth I call you not servants...but I have called you friends,* I had been taught. Some friend I had been.

If we believe not, yet he abideth faithful: he cannot deny himself. I felt myself begin turning from grief to thankfulness. Despite the injuries, I remained, and my purpose in life remained as well. And I had the opportunity to return to my faith.

The fire grew and warmed me. *Thou hast turned for me my mourning into dancing: thou hast put off my sackcloth, and girded me with gladness; to the end that my glory may sing praise to thee, and not be silent.*

I felt a hand on my shoulder, and I clasped it. "I'm okay," I said. I tried to dash away the tears, but my skin burned. So for a time I rested in the grief of my brokenness and the joy of his strength, and in gratitude for faithfulness and the fellowship with Tabitha.

I took a deep breath, squeezed the last tears from my eyes and returned to work, and Tabitha returned to hers. The flame in me, so often ignored and suppressed until it was barely an ember, roared in the hearth of my contemplation. It spoke many more words to me of comfort, security, love, and steadfastness—almost a whole book of them.

And, slowly, as a new fire slowly infuses a room with warmth or dawn infuses the night with color, the emotions began to re-attend to my memories. There was still one glaring gap the night I went to Henri's, but I knew it was an abyss I was not yet ready to peer into. As for the other two things—whatever surrounded Mr. Messick and the Mayor, and who my traveling companion had been—I did not worry about them. When it was time to continue the journey that had brought me to Aurden, those two would come as well. For today I had the simple work of helping Tabitha, and the faculties to do it.

Chapter 10

"Tabitha!" I called. "Can you come out here for a moment?"

She exited the back, dusting off her hands. When she caught sight of me, she froze. "Rae-Anna?" she asked softly.

I was staring at the long table from where she took and sold orders—specifically at the end of it, where a strange whirling star-pattern caught my eye. It was faded, perhaps scrubbed or scratched off. But at the sight of it, the strange childhood tune had begun playing in my head. "This symbol," I said.

"Yes," she replied, but offered no explanation.

I continued to trace it with my eyes, letting my thoughts drift. I had seen it other places: Mr. Messick's, where it adorned shelves and suits of armor and attested to life; at the Mayor's, where it had attested to love. And on a staff and medallion where—I shivered—it had attested to power. "This is what I went to see Henri about," I said. She nodded gravely. My eyes flicked to hers. "You said I went to take him your gratitude."

"I didn't think it would be right to give you a memory you didn't have on your own." Though she said it boldly, her voice wavered. I waved it aside.

"I understand that," I said. "But now I need to see him again."

She looked at me a moment, then ducked into the back. She quickly returned carrying both our cloaks. "I will go with you this time," she said. After we had donned our garments, she laid a hand on my arm. "One other thing," she said gently. "As much to protect your face from the wind..." She trailed off, then reached across and draped a veil over my nose and secured it behind my head. It pinched at first where it lay, then cooled. I touched the veil, my eyes downcast. She stopped just short of lifting my chin, though with her hand cupped below my face I looked up anyway. "You will heal," she said firmly. "Each day it pinks a little more. But if Henri thinks the symbol is at the root of what happened to you..."

"Then throwing it in his face will only make him more frightened," I concluded. She smiled grimly and I nodded. We stepped out into the cold.

Winter was very nearly upon us, and the skies were slate. All the colorful bunting stood in contrast, more fitting for springtime, and the mood of the people around seemed as conflicted. There was still the odd entertainment—a juggler here, tumblers there, an empty stage announcing a mummery to be played later that evening. And so there were spots of laughter or clutches of happiness. Most of the town seemed back about its business. Perhaps the mayor had overplayed his festivities. But it gave the town a half-hearted feel.

We turned at the street and my steps slowed. Tabitha, ahead of me, slowed nearly the same time I did. And yet the alley was empty, and I felt no real threat or menace. Yet somehow we both felt rushing was foolish.

Near his door, there was a strained look to the alley: the dirt appeared swept, a brick wall was missing bits of mortar, and it seemed as if the nearby houses all leaned one way. Such a thing felt impossible, and yet...

Tabitha stepped to Henri's door and knocked loudly. After a few moments there was a scuffle, a few bolts grinding into place, and the final rattle as the latch lifted and the door creaked open. Henri peered out with hollow, haunted eyes that barely softened when he saw Tabitha.

"What are you doing here?" he whispered.

She gestured to me, and I gave a small wave. He swallowed hard, and the haunted look returned tenfold.

"What's she doing here?" he rasped.

Tabitha clicked her tongue. "Henri, please; it's not like she brought it here."

At the strength of her voice he ducked, his finger fluttering around shushing lips. He gestured us quickly inside. As I ducked through I saw him give an odd look down the alley before slamming the door and doing up no less than six bolts and locks. They all looked shiny. New.

"It comes nonetheless," he said. "I don't care who brings it. And you shouldn't either! That doesn't mean we go looking for it, and we don't bring it around a poor old man's home once it's already visited."

"And what is 'it'?" I asked.

He glared at me from underneath bushy eyebrows. "The Insatiable," he said.

I blinked hard at him. I hadn't expected a name. "You're familiar with this thing?"

He looked at me in shock, as though he hadn't realized he'd said it aloud—and then was shocked at himself for saying it in the first place. "Never speak it—never speak it!" he said hoarsely. He wrung his hands. "Never, never, never..."

"Henri," I said, reaching out a hand to calm him. "Please, you must tell me."

"Why?"

I stifled a tremor. "Because that's what I'm here for," I said. "To rid Aurden of it."

"Y-you?" His eyes went wider. "How can you...?"

"Do you have faith in Our Father?"

He took a step back, dwindled, his hands clasping into little acorns. As his eyes darted silently, tears welled in them. He shook his head. "Not since...Not since they came. And I've been under their power for too long. Too long."

"Too long for what?" I asked scornfully. "Too long for Our Father to rescue you? Is His power so easily spent? Can He not fulfill His promise in a moment—no matter how long it was delayed?"

I saw a spark in his eye for a moment, and dared to hope. But it was snuffed easily, and he glared. "I didn't see Him help you very much," he spat.

"Henri!" Tabitha exclaimed. But Henri only sulked.

"If you have not faith, resignation might do," I said. "You just answer my questions, and let me deal with the Insatiable."

He glared at me, and at Tabitha, then flopped into a chair. "Ask."

"Where does the star symbol come from?"

"I don't know."

"Henri," I warned.

He shrugged spitefully. "I don't know where it came from. It is ancient."

"Why are you afraid of it? What is your connection to it?"

He slouched, clearly hoping I wouldn't figure out how to get him to answer. Yet he began: "I was apprenticed to an old carpenter, one who was apprentice when this town was built. He told it to me first. The Insatiable was here when they came to this crossroads, though they didn't know that then. It was only an inn back then—the old inn, on the north-east of the cross."

"That was the one I stayed in when I first arrived," I said.

He frowned sadly. "Then maybe that's why you're caught up in it. Their magic is deep in the stones of that foundation. My old master helped build some of the first homes and shops. The innkeeper, he insisted on blessing each of the foundations—blessing, and marking with that symbol. And to a family, the firstborn always suffered some calamity. Not always death, but always some curse. A twisted limb, a weak eye, a fall from a horse."

"I would think people would begin to distrust the symbol."

"Oh, they did. And the innkeeper would just smile and wink and say it was superstitious nonsense. Then the people began to insist. They tried to refuse the symbol." He swallowed hard. "Worse calamities followed them, and to more than just their firstborn. No one in the family was safe. Stillbirths, deafness, blindness, mindless-ness, insanities. If a family thought they had escaped, that all their children came out strong and healthy, it only meant a worse fate was waiting as they grew older. Until the three Pommier children went out for a picnic and were torn apart by wild beasts. By then my master was a journeyman, and he was there when the littlest arrived back, babbling and out of her mind with skin torn ragged..." He choked off, eyes dripping now. He eventually calmed his shaking, took a few deep breaths. "Eventually, he became a Master and I was his apprentice. The old innkeeper had passed away, and with him the etching of the symbol on everything. No more symbols or blessings—or curses. For a time, we were allowed to forget."

"What changed?"

He shrugged. "It came back. I don't know who resurrected it. By then I had found an old scrap of wood with the symbol on it, barely thought of it twice, and used it to help Tabitha and her husband fit out their shop. I didn't even mention it to them—why would I? By then it held no more power."

"The power seems to have returned," I said.

"I said it was resurrected, and that I meant," he said. "Not just the symbol; I've heard the old innkeeper walking in the dark, checking his symbols."

"Walking in the dark?" I echoed. "With a walking stick?"

"Aye. And always whistling a child's tune."

"But never during the day?"

"No, you never see him," Henri whispered, eyes wide. "You only hear him, hear his stick. And in the morning, someone else is dead or hurt or cursed somehow. Those who believe in him the most..." His eyes flicked intently to mine. "Well, they shield themselves with as many symbols as they can—if they're smart."

I glanced around the room. "I don't see many in your house," I said.

"I'm smarter," he said hoarsely. His lips folded as he shook silently, and tears squeezed from his eyes again.

"How so?" I asked.

But he clamped his jaw tighter and only shook his head.

"Why does the mayor claim the symbol is about love?"

"Because he's not as smart," Henri replied. Distraction seemed to help calm him, though I didn't know what I was distracting him from. "He says so because he only knows love, or some form of it. The young ideal of love, all roses and kisses and midnight assignations. It matters less that you know what the symbol means as long as you have it."

"That seems rather trivial," I said.

"But you are the firstborn, aren't you?" he asked.

I paused. I was the firstborn. But I knew that wasn't why they came after me. I told him so.

"Well, that seems rather trivial," he sneered.

"It could not be less so," I said firmly. "This—you call it the Insatiable; it fears the power I carry with me. Because that power can destroy it."

"I doubt not *you* believe so," Henri said. "I have less faith. So you do what you must. I have done what I must."

I looked at him askance. "What have you done?"

But his jaw was clamped shut again. Somehow I knew it would not re-open.

I turned and left, Tabitha close beside me. She was silent as we walked back toward her shop, her eyes intent on the road. "What's wrong?" I asked.

She glanced at me swiftly. "Nothing, I guess. Strange tales he tells."

"Do you believe them?"

She shrugged. "It seems enough that he does. Perhaps one or two strange occurrences could be explained away. But if he's right? If it was every firstborn?"

"Are you firstborn?"

"No. And maybe I came along after this had ended."

"Until recently. What about your husband?"

She chewed her lip. "Do you know, he was eldest in his family. But his death wasn't an accident, or even very strange. His health had been deteriorating since..." She trailed off, and her hand went to her mouth.

"Since you moved here?" I asked.

She stared at me aghast. "It is true, then," she whispered. "And we came right into the middle of it."

I stopped and turned to her. "Is it true some evil force is bent upon this town, to cause destruction and hold people here under its power? It seems likely. Is it powerful enough to stand up to Our Father and his Sacred Fire?" I snorted and shook my head. "I would love to see it try."

"But it did, didn't it?" she asked, again afraid to look at my face.

"Not truly," I said as we continued toward her shop. "It stood up against me. In my folly I had neglected the Sacred Fire for too long. So when it attacked, it attacked only me."

"Why wouldn't this Sacred Fire still come to your aid? Is it so petty to hold a grudge? So spiteful as to turn away from you?"

"There are times when Our Father will aid someone almost against their will," I said. "At other times, he allows the full force of our freewill to have its way. I cannot say why he chooses one or the other. For myself, I must not think of this Fire as some sort of magical fairy that I only call on in desperation. I must spend time in contemplation, to turn my thoughts and desires away from myself and only to him. Perhaps to remind me, he allowed my freewill full rein for a time. But even that I will not say for certain. All I know is I must be in his presence as much as I can—not just for protection but because I love him. Would you not be with the one you love simply because you love them?"

"I suppose I would," she said.

We turned to enter the shop, and I felt a strange buzzing in my head. Something I had just said resonated like a rung bell. Tabitha went in before me, and as I passed the threshold I leaned my shoulder on the doorframe. The air felt thicker inside, almost as if I couldn't pass through. She proceeded well enough, but when she turned back

I saw her mouth move but heard no words. The buzzing grew, now a pressure in my head. It seemed not to hurt so much as it was simply insistent.

Tabitha took a step toward me, growing concerned. I shook my head. I felt no need to speak. I closed my eyes and prayed, listening for the Fire inside. Despite the battering I seemed to be taking, it flickered not at all. I drank in that stillness, let it spread through me.

Suddenly, almost without prompting for how unconscious the decision was, I turned and looked down the street. They were not many passersby even for Aurden, being near the noon meal, and I could see almost to the fields. And near the end, as my eyes searched for I knew not what, I saw one person who stuck out to me. He was perhaps my age, lean and muscular, with brown hair pulled back in a small tail. I gazed at him for a time, watched him pause near the vendor, Jannis, before he continued further away and eventually disappeared. Just as he turned I thought I saw a sword at his waist—one of the few in the street who did.

I turned back, frowning. He was important somehow, and I had known to turn and look at just the right moment—the Fire had prompted me to it. And I spotted him in the street almost immediately. There was something there...

"Tabitha," I said slowly.

"What is it, Rae-Anna?"

I startled a moment. The buzzing was gone, the thickened air was gone. All sense of wrongness was gone. But there was still something important I had said—what was it? I looked around the inside of her shop. The tableau before me seemed familiar. Except she was in the wrong place. "Can you go stand behind your table, please?"

Glancing at me worriedly, she nonetheless obeyed. I stepped inside, glanced at the symbol, then at her. And in my mind's eye I saw that same young man from the street standing a little apart from me, but knew he waited for me—at least, he waited to speak until I came in. Yet there was a coldness, I couldn't remember why.

"Maybe I shouldn't be here," I whispered. Tabitha looked at me strangely. But that was wrong. "Maybe we shouldn't be here," I reiterated, a little louder.

I saw fear enter her eyes. "What's wrong? Do you sense something?"

But I wasn't looking at her. I was looking at the empty space where he had stood, arms folded, ignoring me. I had hurt him, somehow, and he hadn't forgiven me. He wanted to make his own way, and left me to make my own. And I had, after a fashion...

After a fashion. He was my brother, after a fashion. That's what I had told Tabitha. But he was not my brother. I loved him, and wanted to be with him. Not because he protected me, but just to be with the one I loved. Protection attended him, but was only one facet of our togetherness. He had been with me in the convent when I was fighting the skeletons. He had come with me from Holden. But then suddenly he was gone.

"You said I came here with a young man," I said.

She fixed me with her gaze, and nodded.

"But he's not here now."

Her lip quivered as she shook her head.

I looked through the open door into the street. He had gone ahead of me into the shop. I watched him storm away from me, felt suddenly the tenuous bonds we held as he separated from me so easily. And in desperation I had called after him.

"Thomas!" I said aloud. I turned again to Tabitha, saw the tears in her eyes. "Where is Thomas?" I pleaded. "I need him!"

Chapter 11

We sat at the table, food before us, as Tabitha tried to encourage me to eat. I fought her at first, hands trembling, incessantly trying to turn and rise from my seat.

"We will find him," she said firmly, over and over. "But it will do no good to run about until you collapse. You need to heal, and you need to eat for the strength to do that."

"And if he is starving somewhere?"

"I have never known Mr. Messick to treat anyone in such a way."

"Are we sure he is there?"

She cocked her head. "Why wouldn't he be there?"

I frowned. I picked up the wooden spoon and forced my hand to still, at least enough to get half a spoon of soup up from the bowl and to my mouth. "If he was nearby, and able to come to me, why hasn't he?"

"Well..." She paused and drew a slow breath.

"Unless he doesn't want to see me anymore."

She glared at me. "That is what I was trying to avoid."

I slouched, now, petulant. "Well, it makes sense."

She chewed through a bite of barley bread. "All right, let's use your first assumption then. After all, things in this town have taken quite a turn since you arrived." I snorted, and she favored me with a gentle smile. "You're the one who told me The Beloved called you to this life. And you seemed quite certain."

I sighed. "He did. Maybe it was easier when it was just me." I shook my head; it wasn't. A few memories from the convent shot through my mind. It had been terrible, in the moment. Only at the end, when all had come out right, did it feel justified. "I wonder how this can turn out so that I feel as certain by the end."

"As it does," she replied simply. "Is there some teaching about trials?"

I drew a breath. *"Now no chastening for the present seemeth to be joyous, but grievous: nevertheless afterward it yieldeth the peaceable fruit of righteousness unto them which are exercised thereby,"* I said as the Fire prompted.

She glanced quizzically at me. "Are you being chastened for something?" she asked.

"Apparently."

She looked hard at me. I was being petulant again. I drew a breath. "Let's call it training. Or discipline. It won't be enough for me to just accept this life, surrender to the will of Our Father—or say that I will surrender. I must do it. And the surrender I suspect He'll ask of me in years to come will make today's surrender pale in comparison." I thought back to Sister Lucy, and smiled. "The temptations faced by those with great faith would undo those of us with little faith."

"Do you need to surrender Thomas?"

I considered a moment. The Fire inside did not grow in size, but in intensity. *Whither is thy beloved gone, O thou fairest among women?*

whither is thy beloved turned aside? that we may seek him with thee. I blushed, though I'm not sure it showed through the scars on my face. Fairest, indeed. Perhaps the spoonful of soup I hastily brought to my mouth clued her in.

"So where do we look first?" she asked with the cheekiest of grins.

"The vendors," I replied, fighting my own grin. But as we hurriedly finished our last few bites, the grin faded. It was possible this search would be fruitless, or would confirm my worst fears—that Thomas was gone, either by or against his will. I tamped that down as best I could. It would turn out as it would, and if it didn't make sense by then, it would by the end of the age.

As we donned cloaks once again, I paused. "What about your shop?" I asked.

She looked at me for a long moment before comprehension dawned. "It's Sunday. I forgot to tell you."

I gaped a moment. "And you don't go to Mass?" I asked. How had *I* missed it?

She frowned a moment. "If they're not interested in helping me write my story," she said drily, "then they don't get to know how it ends."

I bit back my reply, knowing it would convict me, and probably more than it would her. I wasn't ready for that. And, perhaps, neither was she.

"Oh. Will we be bothering the vendors, then?"

"I've lived here some time," she reminded me. "They'll understand."

I let her lead the way. By now a pale sun showed behind thinning overcast, a white disc that lent little warmth. What few passersby I had seen earlier were now gone, the streets eerily silent despite the day. Flags snapped in the wind. I thought I heard a brief burst of laughter, like a loud chuckle, but Tabitha didn't react and so we kept on.

Jannis' awning was rolled away and tied to the wall, and there were a few empty crates still on the street. Tabitha knocked on his door, rubbing her hands briskly while we waited. My veil fluttered, tickling my mouth. I glanced at her.

"I know I have no room to say anything," I said quietly. "But Our Father, at least, invites us to return to Him no matter where we find ourselves."

She spared me the briefest of glances, and knocked again. "I have nothing to prove to you," she said.

"It's not for my proof—" I cut off as the door opened.

"What is—oh, Tabitha. And Rae-Anna." His eyes took in my face a moment, then the rest of me. "I had heard something. I am sorry such misfortune has met you in our town. But I am glad to see you...well."

He stumbled over the last. I assumed I did not look as well as I might, so I bowed my head graciously in thanks. He cleared his throat once and turned to Tabitha. "We both know I can sell no food," he said. "How may I help you instead?"

"We wondered if you had seen Thomas lately," Tabitha replied.

His glance barely flickered my way. "Who?"

"Mr. Messick's boy," Tabitha said curtly. "His latest, that is. He has gotten victuals from you..."

She trailed off as comprehension, then consternation dawned. "Am I to keep track of every one of Mr. Messick's hirelings?" he demanded.

Tabitha and I glanced at each other. "Why do you say that, Jannis?"

He folded his arms tightly. "It is cold," he muttered. "And he was here yesterday, as normal. I do not expect him today." His glare bored into both of us with his last statement.

My heart fluttered. "Jannis," I said quietly. Pleadingly. "He means a lot to me. If you know anything—where I might find him..."

"He is not at Mr. Messick's?" Jannis asked. His tone had softened considerably.

I shook my head. "I don't know. He was not there when I called on Mr. Messick, and he has never come to see me—"

"Are you sure he wants to?"

"Jannis!" Tabitha exclaimed. I lowered my eyes.

Jannis sighed shortly. "Go ask the Captain," he said. I believe he hid his shame behind his gruffness. "Thomas had said something about fitting into armor, last he was here. Perhaps Mr. Messick seeks to make a knight of him."

"I'm sorry if we bothered you," I said quietly, looking up just as the door shut in our faces. I glanced worriedly at Tabitha, who glared at the closed door. Finally she turned her eyes to me.

"I don't like what's becoming of our village," she said.

"Perhaps we should forget about Thomas," I said. When she only stared at me, I added: "Shouldn't I focus on whatever it was that brought me here? What is probably causing your village to become what it is?"

Her lips thinned. "Rae-Anna, you stop that right now. For one thing, Thomas is probably tied as tightly in it as you are. No, let's go see the Captain."

The thought horrified me, and I followed her quickly, nearly treading her heels as we made our way down another street. Near the north end of the village, where we had first come in on the road from Holden, she turned aside and approached a squat stone building.

"Our donjon," she said with a slight roll of her eyes.

"Is it that bad?" I asked. It seemed stalwart enough, if laughable in the face of some of the grand castles otherwise dotting the countryside.

She shrugged. "I suppose I'm being unfair. It would keep us well enough in an emergency."

She approached the two guards standing basically upright, though they leaned heavier on their halberds than I had seen some lean on their canes. "We would like to see the Captain on some urgent business," she said.

"Which is what?" leered the first, while the second glanced me over in disgust.

"A missing citizen," she said.

This brought them up a little short; it was a legitimate complaint. After exchanging glances, the second finally tore his eyes from my ruined face and went inside. Presently, a stouter man in marginally finer woolens exited, nodding as he wiped his mouth with a napkin. As the guard returned to his post, the stout man waved us inside.

At first I thought it was the Captain himself. But as he led us silently into the interior my doubt grew. Something of his bearing made me think he had not been in the service long. Even ill-disciplined soldiers did not carry the same swagger as this man.

Finally he came to a large door and banged on it. "Enter" came faintly from within. The stout man turned, smiling at both of us before he sauntered away down the hall. Tabitha only raised her eyebrow when I glanced at her.

When we went in, I beheld the Captain at last. Trim, with a neat mustache and oiled beard, silks, black hair showing some gray, and a sharp eye left no doubt in my mind. "Captain Fontaine," Tabitha said, and I quickly mimicked her curtsy.

"Tabitha," he replied. He examined me swiftly and critically, but said nothing. "May I serve you?"

"We hope so," she said. "We are looking for a young man, Thomas, who may have come to you. I sent him to you a week or so ago for work, and to register..."

"Yes, I remember. Strong man. I sent him to Mr. Messick." Again his eyes flicked to me but didn't remain.

Tabitha smiled. "That part we knew. But we don't know where he is now."

"What has Mr. Messick said?"

Tabitha hesitated. "Well, he didn't. We didn't ask him. But Mr. Messick always lets his boys go after dinner—"

Captain Fontaine's raised hand finally stopped Tabitha's speech as I held back a sigh. It was more complicated than I imagined he had time for. He glanced between us both. Finally his gaze stayed on me. "What happened to you?" he asked.

"Captain?" I said. We weren't here for me.

"Those wounds look fresh—at least, fresher than a week ago."

"I'm fine, Captain—really. Tabitha has taken me in..."

His hand raised again. "That is not what I asked. I know Tabitha's character, especially toward outsiders." I wondered at the tone in his voice, slightly accusatory. "I asked what happened to you."

"It is difficult to explain..."

"Were you attacked?"

I glanced at Tabitha, who gave me the barest raise of her eyebrow. "Yes," I said.

"Here in town?"

"Yes."

"Did you see your attackers?"

"Captain..." I gritted my teeth as his eyebrows arched. I truly did not want to lie—but I knew where his line of query was going, and what was I to say? "Yes, sir, I did."

He paused a moment. "Was it this...Thomas?"

"Oh, absolutely not, Captain," I said hurriedly. "No it was...a group of men."

"Do you know who they are?"

I almost smirked. I knew who they *looked* like; who they were, in their personhood? I glanced at Tabitha again. She shrugged as if to say "why not?" I sighed. "I think they were some of the mayor's retinue," I said. When he gazed blankly at me, I added: "For the wedding."

His gaze grew hard. "Are you certain?"

"I think so, sir. My memory..." I trailed off as his face began to turn red.

"Get out."

I blinked. "Captain?"

"I know what you're about," he continued. "Word has reached my ears too about your attempt at the mayor's decency! And now you would cast careless aspersions!"

I goggled. "Never!"

He rose from his seat. "I've seen plenty of your like," he said. "Never quite so bold as to confront me to my face, but I'm sure it was only a matter of time. You've overstayed your welcome, I think. If I send my soldiers around Tabitha's shop tomorrow, and you are still here, you will stay here—and in our finest and deepest cell!"

"Captain, that isn't fair," Tabitha cut in. "You must hear her out."

"I absolutely will not!" he shouted. "And shame on you for entertaining her wild notions. If not for your husband—"

"Only that?" Tabitha demanded. I didn't like the fire her eyes were spitting.

The Captain ground his teeth. "That courtesy extends only to you, Tabitha. Do not abuse it. She must be gone tomorrow."

"And will your soldiers help me in my shop? Thanks to the festivities I've got five wedding dresses now to sew."

He glanced down at his clenched fists atop the table. After a few moments during which the air nearly hummed, he muttered, "get out."

I glanced at Tabitha, who only gestured toward the door. We went out silently, leaving the Captain in his rage.

On the street as we headed back toward her shop, I blinked back tears. "That wasn't much help," I said.

Tabitha drew a breath. "I certainly had higher hopes when we started," she admitted.

"I don't suppose you want to tell me why you have a hold over the Captain," I said.

She barked a laugh. "Do you remember the tent we talked about, always pitched on the outskirts of carnivals?"

"I—yes, I guess."

"Well, it seems the Captain once frequented those tents. Most unseemly for one of his stature. One belonged to...someone very close to me. Captain Fontaine was horrified when he found out."

"You didn't blackmail him!"

She laughed again. "I didn't have to. He felt some sort of guilty responsibility, swore to me and her he would take care of us both for the rest of our lives. Honestly, I tried to convince him only to take care of her. He doesn't give me money, at least. But he pays a certain amount of deference to me, when it's necessary."

"So do I have to leave tomorrow?" I asked.

She put a hand on my shoulder. "Absolutely not. We have dresses to sew." She smiled at me, and when she looked forward again her smile disappeared. "Oh, surely not."

I looked up and saw another couple at the door to the shop. The young man had his hands cupped to the window, peering in. The young woman hugged herself and stood motionless.

"It is Sunday," Tabitha called out as she neared—not quite frustrated, but clearly put out.

The young man whipped around, then took several swift strides toward us. "I'm so sorry," he said. "But I know the time is growing short. And you've probably so much on order already." He was fairly wringing his hands. His lady remained still, and as her eyes caught mine I saw a haunting I couldn't fathom in a betrothed.

"You are more right than you know," Tabitha said with a sigh. She pursed her lips as she took in the scene. "Well, come in out of the cold, at least. I suppose you want it before the Mayor's own wedding?" she asked as she unlocked the shop door and led us all inside. I smiled at the lady and bid her enter before me. She begrudgingly obliged, her steps slow and timid.

"Not necessarily," the young man said. "I would think it will take time to...um...undecorate?"

Tabitha stared at him. "To take the banners down?"

"Yes, that's it. I don't...I mean, I do well enough I guess. But I'm not beneath hand-me-downs."

"You want to use the mayor's wedding decorations because you can't afford your own."

He winced at her bluntness—I did too, and attributed it to the frustrations of the day. But he nodded.

"Well I can't guarantee the dress will be ready in time, but we'll do what we can. Rae-Anna, if you wouldn't mind?"

"Of course not." I smiled again at the lady, who only looked bleakly at me as I led her into the back. "What's your name?" I asked as I arranged the screens. I was getting quite comfortable with the process, by now, and did it almost thoughtlessly.

"Marie," she said.

I barely heard her as I began measuring. I felt a hollowness inside that I tried to mask, for the sake of the bride-to-be. But it felt like trying to keep a jar from spilling whose mouth is just slightly larger than your hand. I wondered what Thomas was doing, what he was becoming. I knew it had only been a few days, yet an irrational part worried I wouldn't recognize him when I saw him again.

I fiddled with the end of the measuring line. It seemed so certain to be the case—as if I already knew he would be that different. But I had no reason to think so—had I? Or was it I who was so different? Was it my face he wouldn't recognize?

The rustling of clothing pulled me from my thoughts, and I looked up to see Marie re-dressing. "Oh, I'm sorry," I said quickly. "We're not done yet. I'm so sorry; I guess I have too much on my mind." I hurried to begin the next measurement. "Are you nervous for it?" I asked, trying to bring my attention to the task at hand. Thomas would have to wait.

She only shrugged. "I guess. I suppose we'll have time to figure it out."

I raised an eyebrow. "Not a lot of time," I said carefully. "I believe the mayor's wedding—"

"Oh, not that," she said, surprising me by interrupting. "No, the wedding will be fine, I'm sure. It's after that."

"Oh," I said. "I'm sure—I mean, most people figure it out, I suppose." I tried to smile. "Most of us wouldn't be here if they didn't."

She stared at me. "Is that all you think about?"

I flushed hard. "I'm sorry, I guess I'm confused?"

She waved a hand. "It's fine. Just—after waiting so long for someone, it's hard to know if he'll actually make a difference."

I spared a quick glance. She did not seem that old. "I'm sorry you've had to wait," I said. "May I ask: make a difference in what way?"

"You know, if things will actually be any different. From being alone."

I tucked the measuring line away and looked her full in the face. "It's none of my business," I said. "But if you want to tell me, I'm afraid I'm not understanding you from your hints."

Her mouth twisted. "Can I get dressed now?"

I nodded, and turned to put the other implements away.

"My father passed away some time ago," she said quietly. I turned again and watched her. "And my brother left soon after. It's been just me and mother since..." She blinked, wiped her cheek, smoothed her hair. "Mother was fine. She did what she could. But I've been so terribly alone."

"You had no friends?"

She shook her head. "Never for long. They always had other things—other people they would rather visit than me."

"How did you and..."

"Giorgio."

"How did you meet?"

She stood on tiptoe, peering over the screen. I don't know if she caught sight of him or not. "He's a merchant. Well, he's with a merchant train."

"He comes here often?"

She shrugged. "I don't know. I hadn't seen him before."

"Love at first sight?" I asked. I tried to be coy, but I couldn't imagine it.

"That's what he said, at least. But he's—I mean, he should be able to take care of me, right?"

I bit my lip. "What does your mother say?"

She stepped down off the box. "Mother died last month."

The hollowness I tried to cover opened in a chasm. "Marie, I'm so sorry." I reached out and brushed her arm. "I wish there was something..."

"Would you stand with me at my wedding?"

I physically took a step back. "Oh. I...I guess I could. Are you sure...?" My hand went unconsciously to my face. I forgot I still wore the veil.

"It would be nice. I'd feel silly standing there by myself, anyway."

"Can I do anything for you before then?"

"I'll come by later to get you," she said. "I'm sure we can think of something." Though she seemed happier now, there was still a temerity about it, as though she felt it such a fragile happiness.

She exited, and I stayed near the table where Tabitha and I usually ate. While I felt no specific pressure, just having some experience with the emptiness I believed she felt drove me on. And yet, I couldn't recall when I had felt that emptiness. Even on the streets of Holden, before going to the convent, I'd had some people who cared about me. So why did I feel such kinship with her? Was that why I missed Thomas? Was it that hollowness? Unable to manage it myself I needed him to fill it. But could he? Could I truly expect him to? It felt bigger than that.

I folded the screens away, only half-hearing the voices coming from the front. Five dresses to sew—six, now. My brow furrowed. I recalled three customers, plus the mayor, before today. But hadn't Tabitha told the Captain there were five? Had someone come while I was injured? I didn't recall her mentioning it. And there would be five now, anyway.

Something to ask later. I went to the back door, intending to check that we hadn't left any wool to freeze overnight. But as I moved the beam, the fastening came undone and it thudded to the floor. I stepped back quickly, barely keeping my toes from being squished. I sighed, then froze as I looked at the heavy timber on the floor.

Tabitha came rushing back. "Are you all right?" she asked. She looked down, her gaze catching the same thing I did.

Freshly carved on the back side, where we wouldn't see it if it hadn't fallen, was the swirling star symbol.

Chapter 12

"What do you think Henri meant by doing that?"

Tabitha shrugged. "It seems he believes in it."

"So he wanted to protect us? Don't you already have the symbol on your counter?"

"Well it didn't do much good, did it?"

I sighed. "Is this all he was afraid to tell me he had done? It seems harmless enough."

"As you pointed out though, it's odd he had none in his own home."

I scoffed. "That we could see. Perhaps he hid them all, as he did this one."

Tabitha eyed it, then me. "Should we be rid of it?"

I studied it a moment. I felt no harm from it. But when I glanced again at Tabitha, her gaze was locked on it as she chewed her lip. It seemed to bother her more than it did me. "Would you like to be rid of it?" I asked gently.

After a moment her gaze flicked to mine. "I would, I think. I know you say it has no power, but…"

I shook my head quickly. "But Henri seems to have offered it up to whatever power he feels reigns. Do we have anything else to bar the door?"

Tabitha folded her arms. "You seem to believe the power residing in you is protection enough…"

"It is," I confirmed.

She nodded once. "Open the door please?" When I complied, she picked up the beam and unceremoniously tossed it into the evening. She smiled at me. "I feel better about that. I don't like where this symbol is cropping up, and what's happening to those involved with it."

I nodded agreement. Henri was holding back more than I cared for—I still couldn't imagine hiding a carving would make him tremble so. The mayor, in the midst of preparing for his own wedding, tried to seduce me and started rumors blaming me when it failed. And Mr. Messick…

Mr. Messick. The symbol everywhere, including suits of armor. The power at work when Tabitha had arrived, and Mr. Messick also strangely paid deference by the sitting mayor. "Tabitha," I said. When she looked in my eyes, her grin faded. But all I saw was a suit of armor with strange glints in the eye-slit; all I heard was the vendor Jannis telling us Thomas mentioned getting fitted into armor, and the clanking of metal as Thomas departed after his bizarre visit. "We need to go see Mr. Messick right now. I think he has Thomas trapped. And I think he may have re-awoken the Insatiable." I looked at her, saw the fear in her eyes. "Actually," I said, quieter. "This may be something I need to do alone."

She firmed her jaw. "No, I'll go…"

I laid a hand on her arm. "Tabitha, I have what I need in order to face this. And it's why I'm here, I think. You're doing your part by showing hospitality. It will achieve nothing to walk into this danger with me."

Her stare was flat. "You cannot be serious. After everything else that's happened to you, and you expect me to stay here?"

"Then, please, only to get me inside?" I pleaded. "Let me see him alone, though."

I knew the glint in her eye when she agreed. She would do no such thing. But I didn't truly want to argue. Especially as darkness continued to fall. I briefly entertained the idea of waiting until morning. But, by then, Thomas might be elsewhere again—off doing whatever errands Mr. Messick had. And my word in this village was tenuous at best, if I were to start leveling accusations at one of the oldest and apparently most powerful people. No, if I was right, I needed to find Thomas actually imprisoned. The Fire would have to show me how to deal with Mr. Messick if it came down to it.

We made our way quickly down still-empty streets. A few houses showed lights through their windows, but most would not waste the flame if they could help it. The stars overhead were brilliant, though, and I sent my prayers toward them. I didn't know just how much power Mr. Messick wielded, but I would take no chances. *Our Father, protect us.*

When the wicked, even mine enemies and my foes, came upon me to eat up my flesh, they stumbled and fell. Though an host should encamp against me, my heart shall not fear: though war should rise against me, in this will I be confident.

I pulled the bell-rope. Tabitha stood with arms folded against the chill. My fingers twiddled nervously. *My heart shall not fear. My heart shall not fear.*

Sir Jule peered out at us. His grin was hesitant. "It is late, miladies," he said.

"I know, Sir Jule, and I apologize especially for showing up unannounced," I said. "But it's...it is important, sir."

His eyes flicked between us. "What is it about?"

"I was attacked, some days ago," I said. "The Captain of the guard is curious, but I don't know if he can handle it. I thought perhaps Mr. Messick might be able to help."

He bowed his head. "Of course, Lady Rae-Anna. Let me inquire if he will see you."

After he'd gone, Tabitha caught my arm. "Thomas?" she mouthed. I shook my head.

"Not until I know the nature of Mr. Messick better," I said.

A few moments later the door yawned open, and Sir Jule smiled broadly. "Please, enter," he said. "Mr. Messick will see you right away."

"Thank you," I said as we both came in. He shut the door behind us then led us along the same corridors as when I first visited. I peered again, discreetly, at the suits of armor as we passed. None seemed strange, but now the windows behind them were dark. Had I just seen the sun shining through? Was this all a waste of time?

I sleep, but my heart waketh: it is the voice of my beloved that knocketh, saying, Open to me...

I nearly skipped a step. But I trusted the Fire, kept my pace, and reached out lightly with my hand and brushed the breastplate of a suit of armor as we passed it. I felt a quiver like a shock of cold water, and gasped.

Sir Jule looked at me with concern. I brought my hand to my face. "I am sorry," I said. "I thought I had to sneeze."

He merely smiled and kept walking. At the door he announced us, and we stepped inside. Mr. Messick reclined comfortably in the same chair. But there was only one other chair, and Tabitha was still with me. He stopped mid-gesture and folded his hands.

"Sir Jule, bring us another chair if you would." His voice seemed off; had Sir Jule somehow neglected to tell him there were two of us?

"Um, sir," Sir Jule said. I could imagine him trying to struggle with a chair, with his limp. They shared an awkward glance. I felt the strength of The Beloved pulsing through me.

"Perhaps Thomas could help?" I said.

Mr. Messick's eyes glittered through his smile. "A kind thought, but I've said my errand-boys are released after dinner, and what they do—"

"I think they are not," I countered.

Mr. Messick gave a short laugh, though Sir Jule's smile faltered. "My dear, I don't know what you're implying."

"I think Thomas is still here, and I believe—I am certain he is here against his will."

"That is unkind," Mr. Messick said. His smile was gone. "And I think I have been too accommodating already. Sir Jule, would you—"

"No, he will not," I said. "Until Thomas comes with us, we will remain here."

Now Mr. Messick's eyes blazed as his knuckles whitened on the arms of his chair. "And where, pray tell, do you think you come by this authority? You forget this is my domain, and I accept or decline visitors at *my* whim."

His voice had taken on a strange quality, like a voice of many waters. The glittering had nearly gone from his eyes, and the skin around his mouth was pulled tight. For the briefest moment, I thought I saw two pale-red tips flicker between his lips. I took a breath to rest once again in The Beloved—and felt anger surge forward. "You cannot fathom the authority I carry with me," I said levelly. From the corner of my eye I saw Tabitha blanch slightly as Mr. Messick and I dueled with our stares.

Mr. Messick's lips curled into a sneer. "I doubt that, girl. Sir Jule, please see these worms off our premises."

I heard a blade slide from its sheath, and glanced over to see Sir Jule fairly rippling with muscles as he held his gleaming sword at the ready. There was no longer any sign of a gentle man with a terrible limp. Tabitha took a step back, looking to me. I had told her to stay away, hadn't I?

But I turned back to face Mr. Messick. "Thomas will be freed from your grasp, and no man or sword will stand in the way. Are you sure you want to contend with this?"

Mr. Messick's sneer turned into a growl, and he flicked a finger toward Sir Jule. With a shout the knight stepped forward, blade slicing though the air. Just as it was nearly to my head it stopped, clanging harshly against another blade that had appeared from seeming nowhere. Tabitha yelped as one of the suits of armor from the hallway was suddenly in the room, its faceless helm and empty eye-slits boring down upon Sir Jule. Sir Jule strained, face turning red as he attempted to repel the stranger. Though I had an idea who it was. It was my Thomas—and if you'll believe me, he was in shining armor. I nearly let myself be distracted, but Mr. Messick was still in the room. I turned to deal with him.

But before me was no longer Mr. Messick. He had changed, his eyes flat black and devoid of spirit. His skin was thin and cracked as though scorched, and clung to him with no hint of fat and barely muscle. He stood strangely as though unaccustomed to bearing his weight on only two feet. His fingers ended in talons, and his tongue now was most assuredly forked.

"I will keep my prey," he seethed, his voice a dull roar in my ears.

"No, you will not," I replied, far calmer than I felt. "He is already breaking free. And, as I said before, no man or sword will stand in the way of that."

"Do I look like a man to you?" he said, stretching to his full height. His skin gleamed like obsidian as he leered, laced with jagged cracks of red like flame.

"Fair point," I allowed. "Who are you?"

"You would not comprehend it if I told you," he said.

"What do you have to do with the star symbol?"

"I told you before—the symbol is life."

"Your master does not bring life," I said, injecting a bit of my own sneer into my words.

His tongue flickered. "My master brings power, and life is power. I brought it to this creature Messick like I brought it to the man from the Gadarenes."

"Ah," I said. Then, "wait, I thought it was the Gerasenes?"

"It was a region," he said scornfully. "A region can be known by two different names by two different people."

I nodded. "I always wondered. So, you are Legion. I thought you were gone."

He grinned. "I came back."

"You were the innkeeper when Aurden was founded. You've been forcing 'life'—so far as it could be called that—into this body since then?"

"As I said, I have the power to bind, or to free from binding. Do you know they tried to bind the man from the Gadarenes? It didn't work, because I did not desire him bound. The Sisters in Holden tried to bind you. I see that didn't work either."

I rolled my eyes. "I've been over that already. It is true the schemes of The Liar never differ. He is, after all, not creative. But I think you should leave."

I reached out a hand and placed it on his shoulder. His grin lasted only an instant as lines of blood lacerated across my hand. Then he shrieked as his body started crumpling on itself.

"No! Don't send me back there!" he slavered. "You've no idea what it's like there!"

"Nor shall I," I replied coldly.

"No, please, don't!" His bony fingers clasped toward me as he fell to his knees. "You can't. You've seen me as Mr. Messick. You cared about me, didn't you? Would you do such a thing to someone you know?"

"It's time for you to go."

"Curse you! You'll be with me where I am, too, for this! Who do you think you are? You don't have the power to send me there! There's only one man who can send me there!"

I leaned closer and lowered my voice. "Who do you think lives in me?"

His eyes went truly wide, and I saw in them the faintest reflection of a being so beautiful but so terrible, filled with a meaningless power, an authority only temporarily granted. The features in this reflection wavered between irresistible attractiveness and a selfishness so deep that one could instantly sense there was no fulfillment to the promises its beauty made.

I saw it all in barely a blink before the demon possessing Mr. Messick continued to shrivel, tighter and tighter in on itself. The body of Mr. Messick began in some strange way to emerge, but was so emaciated and wrinkled I knew there would be no life left in him. With a final shriek as though the fires of Abaddon had begun to consume—and in truth they probably had—the obsidian eyes went bluish-white and the husk of Mr. Messick lay crumpled on the floor.

I lifted my hand, now restored, and turned. Tabitha was white as wool. Sir Jule sat cowering, thin and with a twisted leg once more. And the suit of armor stood again with the sword-point grounded between his feet, motionless.

"I should have stayed at the shop," Tabitha whispered.

"I did try to warn you," I said.

She swallowed, but despite herself stepped toward the suit of armor. "Is it—is this empty?"

"I believe Thomas is in there," I said. She whirled to face me, and I stepped toward him now too. Gently, in case I was still wrong, I lifted the visor. There, wrapped in steel and appearing asleep, was my Thomas.

"Is he...dead?" Tabitha breathed.

"I hope not," I said. She bowed her head a moment, but still waited for me to do something. I only stared at him. It felt years since I had seen him last. I did not think he was dead; his skin was too flushed for that. But he shouldn't be asleep like this, especially after fighting Sir Jule. And after Legion was banished again to Abaddon. I looked over the suit of armor for the star symbol, but it definitely was not on this one. Unless it was inside...

I came back to his face. He seemed so peaceful. I wondered if that was how he would look in the morning, still asleep. I swallowed, then reached up to brush a lock of hair out of his eyes.

I pulled back quickly as the painless lacerations appeared on my hand again. They faded, then flared again as I reached forward. With my customary lack of understanding, I gently touched his face.

"Let's hope this works," I said breathily.

When I touched him, his eyes snapped open. A thin glaze covered them like a mist of scales. I placed my palm against his cheek, stroked my thumb against a tear that appeared suddenly from his eyes.

"Rae-Anna," he said, his voice broken with a pain I didn't understand.

"Shhh," I hushed him. "I'm here, Thomas."

He moved his limbs only slowly, uncertainly, as though he had been without their use for a long time. He squeezed his eyes shut and open, shut and open. The third time the mist cleared, his hazel eyes shining brilliantly for how clouded they had been before. Those eyes darted around, took in Sir Jule, the rumpled form of Mr. Messick, Tabitha, and—finally—me. He lurched forward a step, and as I withdrew my hand to keep him from toppling on me the lacerations faded again. The sword clattered to the floor as he tossed it aside and yanked the gauntlets from his hands.

I could not tell if he was yet himself, and I continued to retreat as he stumbled toward me, a strange light in his eyes. He tore at laces, ripped pieces of armor off himself as his legs carried him jerkily toward me. "Thomas? It's me," I said, trying to keep my voice from quavering.

The helmet bounced across the floor. The chest plate fell off. All that was left were greaves and boots. His homespun woolens covered him everywhere else. He finally stopped plodding forward and only held out his arms to me. I suddenly realized his intention, and, after too long a pause, rushed forward with a cry and leapt into those arms.

Even without armor he nearly crushed me. "Oh, Our Father," he gasped. "I've been so afraid. I've never known the like. How did you find me? Are you okay?"

He finally loosed his arms enough for me to pull back and look into his eyes. "The Sacred Fire, Thomas," I said, nearly laughing. "How else?"

He smiled too—until his eyes went to my veil. "What's...?" His hand moved and before I could stop him he lifted it just enough to see the rest of my face. The fear I assumed he had been feeling returned to those lustrous eyes—but something else. A hard edge I didn't like, though I'm certain it wasn't directed at me.

"I'm fine, Thomas," I said. "I mean, I'm alive. And still..." I didn't know what I still was, besides alive. "All I can think of is that I've finally found you again. Nothing else matters to me right now."

The anger tinged with sadness, and he pulled me close again. "What happened?" he asked gently.

"This will probably be easier back at Tabitha's shop," I said. Neither of us made a move to loosen our grips, though. "And we still have to deal with Sir Jule," I added.

"No, you don't," Tabitha said quietly.

We released each other and turned to look at her, and at Sir Jule. She stooped over the limp form, the sightless eyes. "He's dead too."

Chapter 13

W e sat at Tabitha's table, sharing a late meal. Night had fallen, but I knew I would not sleep for some time. Between bites, and anytime I could free it, my hand found its way to Thomas' hand or arm. I couldn't let him go again—not out of sight, or out of reach. And so I held on to some piece of him, just to be sure.

I caught him up on what had happened—everything, from the first visitation of the five men with the marked staff, to working and staying with Tabitha, to my various visits. I ended finally with the attack itself—what I could remember—and seeing Henri again.

Thomas rubbed his jaw with his left hand—his right firmly clasped mine, at the moment. "Henri," he said. "He's an old carpenter? Not large but..."

"He waddled," I confirmed after thinking a moment.

Thomas took a deep breath. "He came to Mr. Messick's late one night, when I was...entrapped. They didn't think I was aware of anything, but... Anyway, he came to see Mr. Messick."

"What about?" Tabitha asked.

"Rae-Anna," Thomas said quietly. We waited, mouths agape in disbelief and horror. "He wanted protections," Thomas continued slowly. "In exchange for what he could do about you—or, what he could offer them so they could do something about you."

Tabitha was the first to speak. "Rae-Anna, I'm so sorry. I didn't know he would do such a thing—didn't know he could..."

I waved her to silence. "I didn't suspect him of it either." I turned back to Thomas. "Did he say how he would give me to them?" I asked.

"He said he knew someone, that he could know when you would be coming to visit him and would warn them."

Tabitha shook her head, and rose to take our plates and things back to her kitchen. I watched her go, and as my gaze came forward Thomas was studying me. "What is it?" he asked.

I took a deep breath, cast my eyes down. "I don't know," I said, keeping my voice low. "Usually the Fire warns me about people—gives some indication of evil. But I guess not always." I didn't like that Tabitha had been gone at odd times, seemed often to be hiding something from me, and—what was it Henri had said? The Insatiable whistled a children's tune. Of course he hadn't said which tune, and there were many. And yet...

My trail of thoughts broke as Tabitha re-entered. "Thomas, you will of course stay here tonight. But do you know what you'll do tomorrow?"

Thomas looked at me, and I glanced at her. "Not yet," I said. "I don't know if Mr. Messick was the seat of everything that's been happening here." *Our Father help us if Legion was the least of the problems.* "Perhaps it is over. We'll stay a few days more to see, I'm sure. And I need to help you finish the dresses," I added with a faint grin. "How many do we still have to do?"

Tabitha grunted. "I think just three. Two are done, and the Mayor's should be done in the morning."

We got up to prepare for bed. "I meant to ask, did someone come in while I was injured?"

Tabitha shook her head ruefully. "I all but closed the shop during that time," she said.

I furrowed my brow. "Oh. I thought you had told the Captain there were five dresses to do, but that was before we came back and had that latest couple."

She swallowed, then pursed her lips. "I must have misspoken," she said, smoothing her skirts. She chuckled bitterly. "Or I assumed more would be coming."

I smiled and laughed. "Well you were right," I said. "You have a pallet for Thomas, then?"

"Of course, we'll get something set up. He can stay down here in the work room."

"Thank you so much, Tabitha," I said, perhaps a little absently. She looked at me, and I smiled. "Just tired," I dissembled.

We helped as we could, as Tabitha set up Thomas' sleeping arrangements. She departed with only a brief glance—not wholly of warning, but certainly of caution. I smiled and gave Thomas some proper distance, though I wasn't prepared to go to my own pallet just yet.

"Thomas," I said quietly, eyes down as I picked at my fingers.

"Rae-Anna," he said, his voice comforting. He glanced at the doorway to the front, trading the hug I believe he wanted to give for a reassuring smile. "I thought we would be able to talk sooner than this," he continued. "I couldn't know...but I know I don't want to take things for granted anymore. Like having an opportunity to work through a problem."

"I was so mad at you for a time," I said, my gaze meeting his, though not angrily. "But now I don't know where to start. I still don't know—"

"I know," he cut me off gently. "That was my fault. It's just—I see what The Beloved is doing in your life and I just want to be near to watch His work. Maybe even aid a little bit as I can. But it seemed to me in that moment... Rae-Anna, it is very hard for me to talk about—not just what happened, but how it has injured me. Sometimes I don't understand the hurts myself. And I'm afraid if I talk about it, especially to you, that you won't want to—maybe that's unfair. That you won't be ready to help me the way I might need to be helped."

"Thomas, of course I will—"

"Well it's easy enough to say," he said. Though his voice was gentle, the words stung. He ran his hand through his hair. "Rae-Anna, I don't know how it is with women, with you. But for men...we're supposed to provide, to be strong and faithful and to absorb so much uncertainty without a hint of wavering. My father did, and I've seen others at least seem as though they did. But the things I've seen—things you've seen, what is before us sometimes... I want to be there to see you through, to help you as I can, as I've said. But I can't do it with no support in return. And it seemed in that moment at the inn that you showed no interest in what The Beloved might be doing in my life. In a moment it seemed you had no desire to help. Maybe that was selfish of me. But it's what it was."

"Is that your responsibility though?"

He folded his arms, then quickly unfolded them. "Not yet, of course," he said. "But if we ever become...more than brother and sister in The Beloved, it will be. And I see the life He has called you to and it scares me. A lot. And not the least because of the role I'll have to fill in that life if we choose it."

"What role?"

"That's the point, Rae-Anna: I don't know, entirely. I only know it won't be as simple as tending crops and providing you with a home. And from what we've seen so far, it's going to put us both in more danger than we probably imagined."

Despite the danger we'd already experienced in the convent, I knew he was right. I knew it was asking a lot for him to consider being my husband under such circumstances. "But Our Father will help you fill that role, Thomas, no matter what it is."

He gave me a half-grin. "I know that. But it would comfort me to know you weren't making it harder, as far as you can help it at least."

"I don't know if I can make it any easier," I said cautiously.

His gaze rebuked me. "That's not what I said," he said gently. "I'm not asking you to carry any more of the load than Our Father gives you strength to handle—I would never do that. As I did say, I will even take as much from you as I can. All I ask is that you don't throw more on top."

I gave a tired smile. It's all I had strength for at the moment. "I make no promises against moments of weakness," I said. "Sometimes, I just like your nose."

He cocked an eyebrow, covering his nose with his hand. "Why?"

I shrugged. "It's cute," I said. "Good night, Thomas."

He gave a flourishing bow, keeping one hand still covering his nose. "Good night, Rae-Anna."

I began climbing into the loft. "You better be here in the morning," I called back as I went.

"I will," he replied.

I smiled in the dark as I found my pallet. I found little sleep, though. And just as I began to drift, I heard a walking stick tapping along the road, and a children's tune.

*

The next morning, Thomas was still there—awake already as I descended. He came over as I turned from the ladder. "You don't look like you slept," he said.

I shook my head. "I didn't. It's not over yet. Mr. Messick was not the extent of the evil in this place. I believe he did only awaken it."

Without hesitation, he asked: "Do you know where the other evil is coming from?"

"Sort of. It's from the Mayor's retinue—it has to be. I just don't know how or what to do about it."

"Confront them the way you did Mr. Messick?"

I shrugged. "Maybe. But there were far fewer of Mr. Messick than there were those five." I furrowed my brow as I said it, something nagging at me. But before I could figure it out I heard the bell ring from the front.

"Not another wedding dress," I groaned. Thomas gave me a bemused grin as we headed to the front to see who was arriving so early.

As I feared, another couple stood arm in arm in front of the counter, facing a Tabitha whose patience was worn almost entirely through.

"Of course I can make it," she said. "And I suppose you'll want it before the mayor's wedding?"

"Of course," the man replied. "It needs to be talked about more than any others—I'll have it no other way for my bride."

"There are those ahead of you," Tabitha replied curtly.

The man drew a long-suffering sigh. "Good woman, there is no one ahead of me, not in this village or any around. When can we expect it to be ready?"

Tabitha glanced at the fiancée, sizing her up. She was tall, with thickly braided straw-blond hair draping across shoulders ready to bear the weight of the world, it seemed. "We might have something. Rae-Anna...?" She didn't need to finish. I extended a hand, inviting the young woman into our back room. As I turned, Thomas acted as though to follow me.

"You get to stay out here," I said quickly.

He considered me, then his mouth wagged. "Oh. Of course. Right. I'll stay out here, then."

I gave him a warning smile and stepped into the back with the woman.

"What's your name, milady?" I asked cheerily as I set to work.

"Therese," she said. Her voice was deep for a woman's, but not quite manly. She stripped to her shift with poise, and as one who seemed to have done this before. Maybe many times.

I scribbled, and measured. "Do you mind if I ask how you two met?" I said, adding quickly: "We've had so many weddings to prepare for, it's been fascinating to hear everyone's story."

"Quite all right. It's been a bit of a rocky tale, to be sure. Lots of meetings and partings. You know, life can pull you so many different ways." She paused as she held the line for me. "One might think our stars were quite crossed," she murmured.

I mis-marked the note. I grabbed the blotter, then corrected it. "What made them align?" I asked, trying to not think of the swirling patterns.

Therese shrugged. "Odin, perhaps. Or maybe these things fall into place, or don't."

I tried a light laugh. It didn't sound too forced. "I was thinking simpler, I guess. Why does it work to get married now?"

She gave a small smile. "Be cautious of love, young one," she said.

I looked again, realized that there were lines of wisdom around her eyes. "Sometimes when you think it's gone forever, it comes roaring back."

My notes would be a wreck by the time she was done with her story. This time, at least, I was able to put a small mark through it and re-write it. "I have experienced that," I said softly.

"Hmm. So it was with Allander. He could be such a fool—an overbearing, over-worried, and presumptuous fool."

"So naturally you married him," I said with a wry twist to my mouth. As much of one as I could manage, anyway, with puckering scars.

But she understood, and laughed. "Yes, well, I did warn you about love didn't I? He came roaring back, indeed. All the way from Africa, like a wild lion. Admitted everything I had just told you, but he realized on that far savannah that he could no longer stomach waking up, and I not be there. Without me in his life, he said, nothing made sense. He said..." She paused, and blushed. It surprised me, for how composed she had been to this point. So I let her choose to continue or not.

I finished up and let her get dressed again. As she did the last knot, she turned to me and lowered her voice. "He told me there was an emptiness, about this size—" she held her arms as though cuddling him close— "And without me to fill it, he was incomplete." Her eyes danced as she suppressed a giggle that seemed far out of character. But then, I did not know her that well. I smiled and let her precede me out of the back.

"Well?" Tabitha asked when we exited. I handed her the notes, which she glanced through quickly. "Hmm," she muttered.

"Good woman," Allander warned. She turned on him.

"Your fiancée is beyond fair, but she's massive," Tabitha said.

The room went utterly silent, until she blew out a short sigh. "Mr. Allander," she began again, but Therese actually came to her rescue.

"Which you well knew, my dove, when we met." He glared at her a moment, and she arched an eyebrow. "The better for dumping you on your head in the snow, remember?"

"It doesn't mean she can speak to you in such way," he growled, turning back to Tabitha. For her weariness, she had some fight left, I could tell.

"We won't have any dresses or materials on-hand to even alter," I interjected. "If we had something nearly done, and all we had to do was adjust some measurements, that would be a different matter. As it is, we have to start entirely from scratch. And, as she's told you, we're up to our armpits on other dresses nearing completion."

Everyone now stared at me. I twisted one of my fingers. "It seemed appropriate, since—well, one time I fell into a pond and was struggling to get back out, and the water was up to here…"

A smile quirked Therese's lips first, then Thomas chuckled, and then everyone laughed. "Well," Allander said, "if it's that dire, perhaps we can be patient. Please do let us know as soon as it is finished, and we will make it worth your while."

Tabitha agreed and the couple left. I glanced between her and Thomas and shrugged. "Well, it worked, I guess," I said.

"Just don't go spreading that saying around," Tabitha said. "I'd hate to see it catch on."

"Probably spread like these marriages," Thomas muttered. He came beside me and rubbed his hand down the back of my arm. I leaned into him a moment.

"Their story sounded strangely familiar," I said.

Thomas grunted. "It did, didn't it?"

I glanced at him. "Did you overhear?" I asked, slightly scandalized.

"Oh, no, Allander was telling us about it. Separated and returned?"

"Hm. Yes. But also about their stars seeming to be crossed. It made me think of the symbol again, of Cillian and Siobhan?"

Tabitha nodded, her glance reserved. Thomas hummed. "You're right, he did mention that. Warned me against love, too," he said with a smile. "That when you think it's gone it comes roaring back."

"A rocky tale," I added with a bemused grin.

"Lots of meetings and partings," Thomas concluded.

I frowned at him. "Did Allander say that?" I asked.

Thomas glanced hesitantly at Tabitha. "I thought so...?"

She nodded. "He did. As well as some drivel about 'if she's not there, nothing makes sense.'"

I folded my arms. "I thought that was nice," I said. But even as I said it, something did feel off.

"Sounds more like confusion than love," Tabitha said. "Very common in young men." She gave Thomas a quick but meaningful glance.

"It also has nothing to do with her," Thomas agreed.

But there was something else. Something didn't fit right. "Does it seem strange that their words would match so closely?" I asked. "I mean, their stories, sure—they should. But that they would use the same words?"

They both shrugged. Tabitha said: "Perhaps they talk a lot. Maybe they even finish each other's sentences," she added with a curl to her lip.

I laughed, but damped it quickly. "What did the other couples talk about? Do you remember? The men, when I was in the back measuring the women."

Tabitha took a deep breath and rubbed her face. "Well, the ones before this, let's see."

"Marie and Giorgio," I prompted.

"Right. He talked about loneliness—he's part of a merchant train. Apparently his mother and father died recently, and he had no siblings."

"Love at first sight," I said. Thomas scoffed. I waved him off.

"Hmm. Yes. Couldn't make friends with the merchants, or when he did they would hare off with some other merchant or something."

"And before that? The third couple? Louis and Chloé."

"Yes. Louis. Chloé was perfect as she was. Wouldn't change a thing about her."

"Claude and Loana."

"There was an odd one. Seemed as though he completely changed character as soon as Loana was away. It's not any place to advise anyone..."

"Yes, she too seemed quite capable of handling Claude once she was alone with me."

Tabitha cocked an eyebrow. "He seems to be a bit of a handful himself, actually. Much worse than he was when the two of you were there."

"And—who were the first?"

"Julienne and Maxime. Those two. I wasn't around for them, they were gone by the time I came back."

"Hmm. Still..." I trailed off, running through those days again. Five couples. Five strange men, with a medallion symbolizing life and love. But not life and love the way I would think of it—or the way Thomas would think of it. Not as he had expressed himself earlier. And definitely not the way Our Father ordained it. Twisted, sometimes awfully, but too often more subtly.

I would appreciate your wisdom.

The flame bloomed. *And walk in love, as Christ also hath loved us, and hath given himself for us an offering and a sacrifice to God for a sweetsmelling savour.*

I considered all the ways Our Father displayed His love for us, in and through The Beloved, and thus asked us to love those around us. I quailed a moment as the pieces fell into place. They would be a dangerous enemy, even with the power of the Sacred Fire.

Will I survive this?

And they overcame him by the blood of the Lamb, and by the word of their testimony; and they loved not their lives unto the death.

Overcame by the blood of The Beloved. "We need to find the mayor's retinue," I said heavily. "I think I know what I have to do."

Chapter 14

"He won't see you again," Tabitha said bluntly.

"I can imagine, though I wonder if he knows why," I replied. Thomas stood silently, flexing his fingers on his sword. I hoped he would come with me, for whatever help he could be.

"Can you tell me what's going on?" she asked.

"I won't know for sure until I see them," I said. "Though I believe the five who follow the mayor are influencing the people here, somehow. Making them think they love each other, though they do not actually. Or, not purely."

Tabitha smirked. "Most people do that without being influenced," she said.

I shrugged. "True enough. Maybe there will be more to it. But..."

"You need to see them first," Thomas said quietly.

Something in his voice caught my attention. "Do you know something about them?"

"Perhaps," he said. Slowly he reached up to his neck, fumbled with a cord knotted around it, then drew out a medallion. I gasped as I saw the star symbol on it.

"Thomas," I said, my voice trembling. "You have to get rid of that."

His eyes flicked to mine, then away. "I know," he said. But still he only held it.

"Why do you have it?"

"Mr. Messick gave it to me, when I came to work for him. Said he gave it to all his errand boys, to identify them. Though I guess that wasn't actually Mr. Messick."

"That's how they influenced you, that night," I said. "When you came to see me. It wasn't the armor holding you, it was this. The armor was just, what? Something to hide you in?"

He nodded mutely. And still he only held the medallion in his hand. "I think...I think this might still be useful, though."

"Thomas," I said, inserting as much power into my voice as I could. "We do not fight with the weapons of this world."

His lips writhed a moment. "But I can feel them. I know where they are."

He could lead us straight to them. It would make it easier. And yet... "Thomas," I repeated, a little gentler this time. "We do not fight with the weapons of this world."

His knuckles whitened on the medallion, his fingers closing around the face so the symbol was hidden. A light came to his eyes, a ruddiness to his face, a...youthfulness. Obviously, he was not old. And yet...

It had to be the power of the medallion. I stepped in front of him, placing my hands gently over his. Tabitha sucked in a breath, but I ignored her. "Thomas," I said, now as gentle as down feathers. "The Beloved freed you even while you held this thing. Its power over you is already broken. Any that is left is only what you give it—only what you allow it to have." I gazed into his eyes, only barely noting the lacerations on my hands again. The light in his eyes brightened a moment, then went black. I felt a surge of loathing against me like a physical hand trying to push me away. The Fire went white-hot, as it had at the convent when I burned the bench. The loathing recoiled, and I thought I heard a roar in my head. Thomas bared his teeth, and in one swift movement yanked the medallion, breaking the leather cord, and threw it to the floor. I kept his other hand clasped in mine, barely registering as the medallion burned away and disappeared.

Tabitha took a deep breath. "I didn't think, with the power you two supposedly carry in you, you could be influenced like that, Thomas."

He blinked, studying my hands. "It didn't, not exactly," he said quietly. "I gave The Liar a foothold." His eyes glistened as he blinked away tears. "By harboring anger against Rae-Anna, feeling so self-righteous in my understanding... I'm so sorry."

I brought his hands toward me, touching them to my forehead. He reached out and clasped my head, bending forward to kiss my hair. He straightened, releasing my head, and when I looked up I saw an entirely different light in his eyes. And a firmness, a sense he stood on better foundation now than he ever did before. "I don't know what use my sword might be," he said, "especially since we don't fight with the weapons of this world." He gave me wry smile. "But I still know where to find the mayor's retinue."

"I'm coming," Tabitha said.

I reached out and gave her shoulder a squeeze. "I think that will be a very good idea," I said.

Thomas led the way out, and Tabitha locked the door. "I couldn't handle another order if I wanted to," she said with a grin. I matched it for a moment, until the weight of what we were about to do came back to me.

Thomas continued down the street, his steps sure. I followed in prayer and contemplation, while Tabitha trailed a little behind and to my left. I barely paid attention to where Thomas led us. It didn't really matter anyway. But also I trusted him as much as I trusted in The One who led both of us.

We passed the mayor's house, turning right and nearing the edge of town. Tabitha slowed. I glanced back, chilled by the look on her face. "Thomas, wait," I said.

Tabitha set her jaw. "No. It's fine. Probably appropriate, even."

I raised a brow, but decided to trust her as well. We continued, and at another left turn I saw the fields opening at the edge of town, and a small, nondescript building. The curtains were blood red, and the door was marked with the swirling star symbol.

"What is this place?" I asked as Thomas stopped in front of the door.

Tabitha drew a long breath, then shook her head. "It will make sense soon enough. You're sure this is where they are?" she asked Thomas.

A strange light was in his eyes again—not from the symbol, but as though he understood, and was full of some sort of compassion. And when I looked back at Tabitha, tears glistened in her eyes as she bit her lip.

"You can stay out here, if you need to," Thomas said gently.

She took another breath, unsteady this time, but set her jaw. "No. I feel...I need to go in."

I tried to give Thomas a firm, "we'll talk about this later" look, but when his gaze fell on me that feeling dissolved. I only nodded, and he stepped forward and opened the door.

Before I could see inside, his sword was out and deflecting a blow. I didn't have time to cry out, or the presence of mind to think or say anything. Then he was inside, battling someone, it sounded like, while Tabitha and I stood outside in shock. Finally the blows ceased after a sharp cry. My hand went to my mouth.

"Well, I was right," Thomas called from within. "They're here."

I only allowed myself a short sigh of relief before I entered. His part of the fight was over; mine was about to begin.

It was, not surprisingly, dimly lit inside. Thomas stood over a man who cradled his right arm, rivulets of blood streaming down to his elbow and dripping on the floor. But he was not entirely my concern. Across the room, the mayor was just rising, his mouth gaping in surprise. His five retainers surrounded him, unprepared but it seemed they were unconcerned. A woman sat across from the mayor, clutching at her bodice and trying not to cry.

"What are you doing here?" the mayor demanded, glaring at me. "Come for another try?"

But I paid him no attention. My gaze was on the leader of the five, and the staff he carried in his hand. They were The Insatiable, I imagined. I addressed the leader. "You know why I'm here."

He gave me a leering smile. "Of course I do. They all come to me, in the end."

I scoffed and grinned. "No," I said. "Not quite."

A moment's hesitation froze his smile. The other four shifted, took more aggressive positions. But they did not move toward me. "Is that sssso?" he said, his tone of a barely-controlled attempt at curiosity.

"Do you know I've already taken care of Mr. Messick—or, what was inside him?"

The mayor looked horrified; the four looked to the fifth with mild alarm. The fifth glared. "His subtleties would never last. They never do. But they were useful enough in awakening us."

"Not like yours," I mocked.

Now the fifth took a step forward. "I think you know not what you play with, girl."

"Kilvan, what are you two talking about?" the mayor asked.

Kilvan paused, glowering. His smile returned. "Nothing, my friend. Just a delusional young—"

He cut off as I strode forward, hand outstretched. "Be silent," I commanded as the lacerations appeared. Kilvan hissed, his lips pulling back, stretching all the way to the hinge of his jaw as his long tongue writhed at me.

"Kilvan, what—?" The mayor began. Kilvan turned and backhanded him.

"Ssssilence! You pestilence—" He cut off again with a strangled growl as I reached him and grasped his arm. He cried out as smoke rose from his sleeve, and wrenched himself free. "How dare you!" he shouted. He raised his staff as though to strike me.

Appearing again as if from nowhere Thomas leapt in. The staff cracked against his sword, and the five startled as if struck. Thomas lashed again, and the head of the staff sheared off and bounced across the floor. The girl shrieked, covering her head as she ducked.

But the symbol was just a focal-point for the power of The Insatiable. Kilvan threw the staff away, and the five took bracing postures. A torrent of emotions and thoughts battered against me, almost as they had when I was at the mayor's house for wine. Behind me I heard Tabitha groan; she was probably under the same assault. But unlike at the mayor's house, all that battering came to me in a distant way, as though they knocked on the door. All I had to do was not answer it.

"You made two mistakes in your pride," I said calmly. Their eyes rolled as they realized I was not being affected by their assault. I continued: "The first was to show yourselves too soon. If you had not come to my room, I might have missed you all entirely."

"And the second?" Kilvan's teeth grinded, his fists in tight balls.

"You attacked me outside Henri's," I said. "Because you wiped out my memories for a time, it caused me to reconsider all the 'lovers' coming to Tabitha's all at once. Without that I may not have put it together."

Almost comically, they kept up their barrage as though Our Father's protection was a barbican that could be battered down. I ignored Kilvan for the moment and walked over to the first—and, I deemed, the least—Insatiable. "You, I name Lust," I said. "You make people think beauty and attraction are the source of love. That if they swoon hard enough, it's the real thing. But the *base things of the world, and things which are despised, hath Our Father chosen. For Our Father seeth not as man seeth; for man looketh on the outward appearance, but Our Father looketh on the heart.* Therefore you are a lie." I pressed my lacerated palm against his head. With the hiss of indrawn breath, Lust collapsed, his robe crumpled on the floor as his horrible and twisted form writhed and disappeared. The battering lessened.

"You are Control," I continued, facing the second. "You cause those who think they love to use it as a means to acquire. They think they are what is best for the object of their desire and lord it over them. They stifle and oppress in the name of their love, and the end of that person is worse than the first. But *greater love hath no man than this, that a man lay down his life for his friends.* Therefore *let this mind be in you, which was also in The Beloved: he made himself of no reputation, and took upon him the form of a servant.* You have no place in love." To his credit, Control tried to escape. But almost against his volition his arm reached out, the cloth of his cloak stretching for my lacerated hand. He, too, burned and disappeared in his ruined shape.

"You are Acceptance—perhaps the most devious," I said. I sighed heavily. "You make people believe that love means they can think and do whatever pleases them. The mere suggestion of discipline, of a way of living that Our Father built into us and into the world, is hate. To call someone to a higher, purer, holier existence is cruel. And, without the aid of Our Father, perhaps it is. But to ignore potential, to ignore the damage someone does to themselves, is not love. But *whom the Beloved loveth he chasteneth, and every branch that beareth fruit, he purgeth it, that it may bring forth more fruit.* None of us are born as we should be, therefore all of us are called to seek and pursue the will of Our Father. You are the true hate." Before I even finished I gripped him, felt the power roar out of me and gut him. He popped with a sound like snapping fingers, his form a mere wisp before his cloak hit the ground.

I moved slowly to the fourth. "You are Emptiness," I said sadly. This one, I knew—not only had I felt his power at the mayor's table, but we were intimate from the time my parents turned me out until I realized what the Fire was in the convent. "You make people think that a person, a simple human love, can fill a void in their hearts. That if something is missing, all they need to do is find a person who can bridge the gap. They drain each other, demanding from their fellow man what can only be given by Our Father. *But Our Father shall supply all your need according to his riches in glory by The Beloved.* For *we are crucified with The Beloved: nevertheless we live; yet not we, but The Beloved liveth in us: and the life which we now live in the flesh we live by the faith of The Beloved, who loved us, and gave himself for us.* Your love, predictably unfulfilled, turns to hate and infidelity." I shook my head, touching him to make him go away. His form was bloated and grotesque, a caricature of satiation.

"And you," I went on relentlessly to the leader. Kilvan panted, all his worshipers gone but unable to leave of his own will. I stared at him for a long time. "You are Selfishness."

"I cause those who would ignore their own needs to value themselves, to find worth in themselves, to keep from being trodden upon—" He cut off in a strangled gargle as I held up my hand.

"But yours is the twisted way," I said. "And in love you have little place. Your love is one that looks to your own needs, how the object of love fits you, changes you, supplies you, benefits you. You feed on the need for others, for community, but use it for your own ends. But that is not why Our Father supplies our needs, nor why He loves us."

"So, what, then?" he sneered, fighting past the strangling power still surging from me. "Your love also empties, makes people give everything, with no hope of return. Ahhh!" He squeezed his eyes shut, his teeth gnashing. When he finally forced his eyes open again they were bloodshot and fiery. "You would have people think they are worthless unless they serve you. Hated. That they are a mere tool. That they are loved only if they perform the way you want—!" His voice cracked and finally failed, though his eyes continued to bore into mine.

"I think you've been spending too much time with your friends," I said. "True: fallible people take advantage, if they can, of innocent love. Which is why we must also be wise. But when Our Father says that love *suffereth long, and is kind; envieth not; vaunteth not itself, is not puffed up, doth not behave itself unseemly, seeketh not her own, is not easily provoked, thinketh no evil; rejoiceth not in iniquity, but rejoiceth in the truth; beareth all things, believeth all things, hopeth all things, endureth all things*—He tells us these things not to place a heavy burden or impossible task on us, but because it is the nature of His love toward us."

When I laid my hand on him, his skin writhed as though it encased a viper's nest. For a moment my hand trembled, and I felt a fire like harsh lye spreading down my hand. I quailed a moment in fear, but the flame rose up. I looked on this person, realizing he was probably possessed by some demon as well—they all had been, as Mr. Messick had. I wondered how they had gotten that way, what their lives might have been like if they had not succumbed to evil, and my fear quenched in pity.

Much as I had scrubbed the corners of the dormitories, I felt the Fire and the Blood scrubbing the poison away from my hand, pushing it back into the demon. His eyes went nearly lidless as his mouth opened in a soundless scream. His skin now felt like it was boiling underneath, and yet I did not need to keep a grip. The blood from the lacerations coiled themselves around his arm and the boiling and writhing fled before it.

Finally a brief, high-pitched scream only barely longer than a squeak erupted from his mouth and he collapsed, leaving me holding his cloak. His skin wrinkled and folded in age, his eyes went blue and then milky-white and the palest of breaths left him as he died. I opened my hand, letting the cloak drop.

There were a few moments of silence, and Thomas came up to me. "What happened to your hand?" he asked gently.

I held it up and inspected it, still lined in blood. *"But he was wounded for our transgressions, he was bruised for our iniquities: the chastisement of our peace was upon him; and with his stripes we are healed."* I paused, nearly reaching under my veil to my face. Would he heal me, too?

I bear in my body the marks of Christ.

My fingers curled shut and I lowered my hand. Not yet.

"Everything you talked about," Tabitha said quietly, tremulously, behind me. "About love. It sounds like that love is less concerned about the past than about potential."

I turned to Tabitha, to see how she fared through all this. But the woman behind me was not Tabitha. I took half a step backward as she lowered her eyes. Then I looked closer.

It was her, but older by perhaps twenty or thirty years. I hissed, taking a step forward with my hand raised again. "You *are* part of this!" I said.

"Rae-Anna, no!" Thomas called. "Wait, look."

I turned on him. The girl that had been sitting with the mayor was trembling and weeping, now suddenly older than me. And the mayor, too, had aged by a decade. He looked at me somberly.

"Welcome to Aurden," he said huskily. "A village that time suddenly remembered."

Chapter 15

I rounded again on Tabitha. "Did you know all this?" I asked.

She shook her head mutely, a tear trembling on the end of her nose.

"She doesn't," the mayor said. "None of us did, while it was happening."

"But, you just said—"

"And she knows it now, too. I imagine every villager realizes it now."

"I believe them," Thomas said quietly. "I felt it under Mr. Messick's power. Nothing seemed wrong while I was under the spell, or whatever it was. But as soon as you woke me up I understood all of it."

"What is this place, this house?" I asked. "Is that part of what you understood when you woke up?"

"No, I'm not sure where that came from." He glanced at Tabitha. "But I'm right, though, aren't I?"

Tabitha cast her eyes to the mayor, then back at me. "I'd rather not talk here," she whispered.

I was still shocked by this change in her. She had seemed full of confidence before. Was it just the change now that the Insatiable were gone? And if everyone was oblivious to it all, why did Henri seem to know so much?

I looked at the mayor and the not-as-young woman. "You may as well go," he said with a wave of his hand. "Much will need to be done for the village in the aftermath of this...thing. Probably many who will be found dead." He rolled his eyes at me as though it were my fault, his lips pressed tightly together.

"I can imagine," I said coolly. "Sorry to have set you free from oppression—you and your village."

He stood up with a sigh and slid by Thomas to get to the door. He paused after opening it. "Don't expect a hero's welcome," he said. "I think most of us were happy. Near-eternal life?" He shook his head. "It's going to be hard to give that up."

"Near-eternal life here," I agreed. "But now you and your people can choose actual-eternal life in Our Father."

He snorted and walked out.

"I should still wait here," the not-as-young woman said quietly.

I opened my mouth, but Tabitha spoke first. "You absolutely must not," she said. Both of us stared at the vehemence in her tone. She shook her head and cleared her throat. "Tomorrow, come to my shop," she told the woman. "I will have much to tell you. Promise me."

The woman was nodding jerkily, quailing under the force of Tabitha's voice. But Tabitha only returned the nod calmly, turned on her heel, and led us out of the strange house. When we reached the shop once more, she let us in and locked the door again behind us. We went to the table and sat.

"Do you believe me that I was aware, but not fully aware, the whole time you were here?" she asked first.

I paused, glancing at Thomas. He gazed at me steadily. "I will," I said. "Stranger things have happened to me," I continued wryly. "I will believe you enough to hear your story."

She nodded. "Then, perhaps let me begin with something you already suspect." She paused for a breath. "I was the woman you saw in the tent outside the carnival."

Of course it made sense, after all that had happened, but it still shocked me. "What about everything you told me when I asked?"

She shrugged helplessly. "Most of it was true. I did have a husband, we met...after the events I'm about to tell you. We came here and opened the shop. He became ill and died. And everything else about my life here—all true. But before that...When I was telling you, I thought it was the truth. I only realize now I lied to you. I don't know how the power here worked—do you?" She asked it pleadingly, but I could only shake my head. She sighed. "I'm afraid the mayor is going to prove very right," she said. She shook her head as a tear formed in the corner of her eye. "There were so many lies I hid behind these past weeks, and now the truth is flooding back I—I don't want it! I wish so badly to go back to the way things were." Her hand trembled as she wiped her mouth. "My head knows not to blame you, but my heart..."

"What lies?" I asked gently.

"There was some truth within everything I told you," she said. "Truth about how women like that—like me—managed to keep our lives together. Ways to keep ourselves alive and...in business...even after learning we were pregnant."

I nodded, remembering our conversation, then froze. "Oh, Tabitha..."

Her eyes glistened. "For years I was able to forget. It wasn't me, remember? It was other women like that. I knew about it, but certainly not from experience. But something inside me started to change when we went to that house..."

"What was it?"

"It's labelled an apothecary, but that symbol...the color of the curtains...marks it as a very special kind of apothecary. It's where you can get the work done."

A fear invaded me. "Thomas, how did you know—?"

He shook his head, cutting me off. "Not because of that," he said. "Something whispered inside me, encouraging me in a way. It was—"

"The Sacred Fire," I finished. I was somewhat familiar. I turned back to Tabitha. "I'm still surprised you were able to tell me anything without threatening the power," I said. "You helped more than anything in pursuing and unraveling the mystery."

"It was you," she said. "You gave me a strength to push past some of the...inhibitions. I don't know what to call it. But I felt it even if I didn't know it."

"Felt what? That you needed to help me?"

She shook her head, her eyes watering anew. "You know, when you need services like that place, all you see in the moment is the fear, the uncertainty—or, rather, the certainty that you can't do it. There's no possible way. It will be too much of a burden. It'll keep you from being able to survive. That your future is more important than—" She cut off with a gasp. "Oh Rae-Anna, I think she might have been like you, if I hadn't—and I wished I had let her live long enough to find out."

She was sobbing now, and I got up quickly and wrapped her in my arms. I didn't know what to say, if there was anything to say. And so

I only held her, and maybe that's all there was anyway.

After a few moments, she kept talking into my shoulder as though she hadn't stopped, though her voice was stronger now. "No one reminds you that one day the burden and uncertainty will be over. One day, that burden and uncertainty grows up into something like you." I pulled back and gazed into her eyes. She continued. "There's always a way, isn't there? I wish someone had told me. I don't know if it would have helped, if I would have listened back then." She shrugged miserably. "Maybe it only makes me feel better, to blame them instead of myself."

"There's no need to blame," I said gently. "Blame and guilt doesn't change the past, and only repentance changes the future—but I think perhaps you've done that."

She wiped her eyes and looked at me quizzically. "How could I? I can't have another child, now."

I smiled. "You had me," I said. "And you had every opportunity and reason to throw me out and abandon a responsibility toward me. But you didn't. Even under a spell."

She nodded, but hesitantly. "Do you remember what I asked you earlier? About the kind of love you were talking about?"

"Yes," I said.

"Was I right?"

"I believe so," I said. "When I consider Our Father's love for us, what it compelled him to do, it was all because of what we could be, not because of what we had been. In ancient days the sacrifice was made *after* the transgression. The Beloved came and sacrificed himself even for those who will never accept him. He sacrificed for the chance that we might, not the assurance that we had."

She took a shaky breath, and smiled. "I might have to start going to Mass again."

I smiled as well. "I do recommend it."

She wiped her eyes again and cleared her throat. "Thank you, Rae-Anna," she said, then sighed. "I must look a fright after all that. Will you excuse me a moment?"

"Of course, though you've never looked more beautiful," I replied.

Her smile thanked me for the compliment, and she rose from the table.

"Tabitha," I said quickly. "You called her a 'she'...how did you know?"

She paused a moment. "I didn't—not for certain, of course," she said quietly. "But there were times...haunting times, where I was sure..."

I held up my hand. "That's enough," I said. "I am sorry."

She gave me a tight smile and departed. I watched her go, then looked at Thomas. He still seemed troubled. "What is it?" I asked, laying a hand on his shoulder.

He picked at a loose grain on the table. "Just, a little bit of what you said just now," he replied. "I think...we should talk."

"About what?" I asked. I tried to keep my voice light, but failed.

His eyes darted. "About being wed."

I sat heavily. "You too, now?" I asked, attempting a smile. When he didn't return it, I continued in a quieter, more serious tone. "What changed?"

"A few things. Being trapped, away from you. Knowing we're going to continue to travel together, and it will be fair easier as husband and wife than as brother and sister in The Beloved."

It wasn't exactly romantic. But he meant it, I could tell. "What about the other thing?" I asked quietly. "This won't fix it."

His eyes darted to mine. "I know it won't. But, like you said, love is about seeing the potential, not the past. I think with you, what The

Beloved has called you—called us—to, it will be far easier to pursue that potential together than to keep being blinded by the past."

I considered him a moment, then made one last attempt at levity. "Is it okay if I still think your nose is cute?"

He glanced at me sideways and grimaced. "I think I'd like it better if it were handsome. Noble, maybe even."

"Hmm." I tapped my chin in thought. "I wouldn't."

He smiled and shook his head. He looked at me with those beautiful brown eyes that seemed to suddenly drink in my features. I blushed, thankful in part for the veil that still covered me. And my smile faded. There still seemed to be no healing for me.

His hand was on mine as if he sensed my feelings. "Rae-Anna," he said softly. I gave him the briefest glance. "If I had wanted a spouse with immaculate make-up and elaborate dresses, if that was what I thought was best and most beautiful, would I have been looking in a convent in Holden?"

"I don't need to be immaculate," I said bitterly. "But do I have to be ruined?"

I looked up in time to see pain flash through those eyes of his. "So you carry your hurts on the outside," he said. "Mine are inside. Am I ruined too, then?"

"Oh Thomas, of course not! That's…" I almost said 'different.' I knew he wouldn't see it that way, even though I did.

"What do you think of me, then?" he asked. "Am I a good man? Worth being married to?"

"*I* think so," I said. "You've no idea how much I missed you, felt torn apart inside worried our fight would never be mended…" I trailed off, realizing what he was saying.

He nodded. "Then accept the fact that I think you are beautiful enough to be married to—for every part of you, inside and out."

I shook my head. It was too hard to believe. But he had a way of doing that—seeing me in ways I never saw myself. I sighed. "I'll try."

He lifted my hand and kissed the back of it, and I blushed again as I felt the gentleness of it. "We still have a problem," I said. He blinked. "I don't think I can convince Tabitha to make me a dress. We've so many to make already, and..."

I startled as the floor behind us creaked. Tabitha walked in with a smile. "Forgive me, but I only overheard the last part."

"Tabitha, please, you've done too much already," I said.

She laughed lightly. "You're probably right." She went to the closet she had always kept shut and emerged quickly with the most exquisite dress I had ever seen. Granted, I had not seen many, but even so. I gaped.

"Was that yours?" I asked.

"No, I've been working on this for you since just after you arrived."

I stared at her. "All the times you were gone without warning, the putting things away just as I would walk in..." I shook my head as she beamed. "But how did you know?"

She shrugged. "I saw things between the two of you I don't think you noticed," she said slyly. I glanced at Thomas, who looked at the ground. "Even when you two were fighting, I saw the way he looked at you." She shrugged again. "And I knew."

I looked at Thomas, who gave me a small smile. I reached for him, and his fingers entwined with mine as he stood. "Well, one thing is settled for sure," he said. "You will definitely look beautiful in that dress."

I looked the dress up and down, and couldn't help but agree.

Chapter 16

Though that was settled, there was much that was not. We needed a place, a time, and a priest. For the rest of the day, I assumed that would take us far longer to arrange than it did.

As it happened, the mayor's fiancée found out about the woman at the special apothecary. While I suspected Tabitha, there was no real evidence. His fiancée also heard the truth about me, and the false accusations Paulo had made to cover up his own faults. But again, there was no real evidence. And, as it also happened, it was her father's demesne on which they were to exchange vows.

Since the priest was already expecting to oversee their marriage, he was more than pleased to oversee ours. And since the entire town had been expecting to attend a wedding at that time, they too were happy enough to show up for ours. They were not nearly as disgruntled at being set free from their dream-state as the mayor was, but then he had lost far more power because of it than they had.

And so I found myself standing at the outskirts of a throng, the sun far overhead on an unseasonably warm day—I could only imagine it would be the last of the year. The banners and streamers and smiling people and bouquets and nosegays were suddenly for me, for a day I had thought wouldn't come for months yet. If not years.

Thomas stood up ahead, waiting by the arbor with the priest. He had not yet caught sight of me. But I trembled. My first test outside of the convent and I had been scarred, as far as I knew irredeemably. Despite everything Thomas had said, it did not seem fair to him. We had every expectation that he would be healed of the hurts inflicted on him by Judith. There was no reason to expect my face would ever look as it had. And one particular scar near my mouth still pulled uncomfortably, preventing my lips from drawing together the way I wanted. The way I would need. My veil would hide me until the last moment, but that scar would be there forever. And Thomas didn't know, yet. We had never kissed. I expected it to be awkward anyway, the first time. Now I wasn't even sure he would be able to figure out how to manage it.

I thought of running. I could go south without him, let Mahmoud catch up with me whenever he did. This was my life, my calling to pursue. I made it harder by having Thomas along. He didn't want me to make it harder, he'd said. And I would not even be a good wife for him. I would drag him from terror into terror, for only selfish reasons. So my heart ached for him; good for me. He had supported me, saved me more than once, been my literal knight in shining armor by happy accident. Women would be envious of me when they heard. My mother would be proud. Maybe.

Would the men envy Thomas? Married to a disfigured wife who would not even keep a house for him? Couldn't provide children for him, with the life we had been called to? Could not even give him a proper kiss?

This could not work. It was a ridiculous idea. He thought he was being noble by what he did. But we were both fools. Worse than any of the other couples who had showed up at Tabitha's dress shop.

But God hath chosen the foolish things of the world to confound the wise; and God hath chosen the weak things of the world to confound the things which are mighty; and base things of the world, and things which are despised, hath God chosen.

I shook my head. *Please not now, I'm trying to mope.*

Thomas saw me, now. And, The Beloved help him, he was grinning like an idiot. An idiot who still thought I was beautiful. Worth marrying. I sighed and stepped forward. *Answer not a fool according to his folly,* I thought.

Tabitha broke off from the crowd to attend me. She had not provided a long train, but there was some small arranging to do. She stepped back, and I faced Thomas through the veil. There was a moment of silence.

"You are Rachel, not Leah?" Thomas asked. I appreciated the silly grin, but I feared he would not find me to be the Rachel he hoped for.

The priest droned on. I knew the language from my time in the convent; I doubted the rest understood any of it. Our Father would translate it into their hearts. *As The Beloved loves the Church. As the Church submits to the Beloved. Giving honor unto the wife as the weaker vessel, and as being heirs together.* Thomas and I exchanged a look, as though remembering our individual weaknesses put on display these last weeks. But I knew what was meant: the expectations of society put me at a disadvantage, and he needed to be aware of it. I knew he was.

There was more, but all of it sped by in dreading the upcoming moment. We managed to repeat the parts we were meant to, took communion properly, and all the rest. I wondered if the mayor had intended to go through all the traditions. Probably, for appearance's sake at least. There was the briefest of moments, with the wafer on my tongue, that all the dread fell away. I couldn't help but glance sideways, recognizing we partook of The Beloved simultaneously. Thomas' Adam's apple bobbed as we both swallowed the Eucharist, and the most important words had gone through my mind. *Therefore shall a man leave his father and his mother, and shall cleave unto his wife: and they shall be one flesh.* With everything else that had happened across the past month, between Holden and Aurden, I wondered how that passage might manifest itself. I hadn't known the Sacred Fire to manifest so boldly, and I wondered if our new life would similarly display itself in some way.

But then we were returning to our positions, and the priest said a few things more. The crowd responded in kind, though we would probably be journeying on and their promises meant little. And yet, as I caught Tabitha's eye, I wondered. She had fulfilled the declarations already. I hoped we would return to Aurden one day to check in on her. Some tears of joy sprang unbidden as I smiled.

There was an expectant silence. I returned to myself, managed to realize what the priest had just said. I turned to Thomas as my smile faltered. I took a shaky breath as I managed to look into his eyes. He gently lifted the veil as my heart screamed at me to run away. Somehow I did not.

As he moved toward me, my eyes burned with tears—not of joy, now, but fear. I could feel the tug of the pocks and scars on my lips that wouldn't move the way I wanted them to, needed them to for the sake of this kiss. My eyes fell. There was an echoing silence from the crowd. But Thomas gently touched my chin, brought my gaze unwillingly to his.

"Trust me," he said, his smile barely more than a grin but conveying a warmth to rival any hearth. "I see you."

He bent in, then, and as I closed my eyes his lips conformed themselves to mine, even in their brokenness.

The crowd roared in celebration, Tabitha told me later. But I didn't hear it over the joy in my heart.

*

The following day, the couples showed up in batches to cancel or postpone their weddings. It was still shocking to see who had aged and by how much—probably more shocking to them to see that their potential spouses were suddenly as much as thirty years older. The evil that had invaded Aurden seemed to vary in its effects, perhaps as people let more or less in.

I spent some time with Marie, the fiancée who had felt so lonely. Her story had some truth as well: both her parents had died, had been the first-born in their families. It seemed The Insatiable did take those as sacrifice. It infuriated me how they had so grotesquely copied the ancient Law, but without the option to redeem sacrifices that Law provided. It had somehow instead fed their power, that the lives they took could be given to those who would worship them.

Near evening, we received news that Mahmoud had returned, his mule laden with his efforts to the east. Thomas and I went out together to meet him. My hand unconsciously found Thomas' and we laced fingers.

"Welcome back," I said. "We missed you."

His eyes shifted between us, then flickered down to our hands. "Indeed."

"Seems you were able to conduct your business," I continued, gesturing to his packs. "Do you need rest?"

He hesitated. "I think we must continue south."

"I mean, it's just for a day," I continued, with a glance at Thomas.

"You must be tired from the road?"

His dark eyes glittered as he looked at the banners and flowers still bedecking the town. "Not so tired," he said. "Perhaps I will continue. You may catch up later. We will not make the sea before winter comes."

I narrowed my eyes. "Mahmoud," I said cautiously. "Are you nervous about something?" When he didn't answer, my eyes went wide. "You knew, didn't you," I said.

He looked uncomfortably between us. "I did not know. I worried. It had been a long time since I came through here, but nothing had changed. Not even the innkeeper."

A little ember of anger lit inside me, distinct from the flame I was used to. "And you left us here?"

He stared at me levelly. "Your Father was not powerful enough to protect you?" he accused. "That is not the confidence you displayed in front of your convent."

Thomas' hand left mine as he stepped forward. I had never noticed before how much taller Thomas was, and broader. Physically, he was only slightly taller than the Moor; I cannot say the same about the mood he projected. "You might have given some warning," Thomas said.

Somehow, Mahmoud stood his ground, staring up at Thomas unblinking. "What would you have me say? The innkeeper had not aged?"

"You might have given us some warning."

Mahmoud's piercing gaze found me. "Unless I am mistaken, she had warning enough."

He was right. Nothing he might have said would have prepared us more than when The Insatiable found me that first night. I laid a hand on Thomas' arm. "It still might be helpful next time to let us know anything you see, Mahmoud," I said. "You've been in these lands before."

He bowed his head once, glancing up again as Thomas finally backed away a step. "This thing—it is gone from Aurden, then?"

"Completely."

He stood a moment longer. "I would still prefer to go south. We must reach Fosse before the snows."

I had not heard the name before, but when he said it I involuntarily glanced at Thomas. His jaw was set firmly, too, as he shared my look. I took a deep breath. "Then let's be on our way," I said.

Mahmoud glanced between us again. "This means something."

"When the snows come, we'll be stuck in the castle, right? No haring off for other merchanting opportunities?"

He shook his head, now clearly worried.

"Then it means, Mahmoud, you will finally see a display of Our Father's power."

*

We left Aurden, not hurriedly but quickly. A cold wind blew behind us, pushing us and scattered dried leaves and barley stalks. What warmth I found was in Thomas, in the knowledge that the Sacred Fire had freed a village—not just me, or a convent, but an entire people. Though not all had come to The Beloved, some had. And the rest, I deemed, were freer now to do so than they had been.

Of course, we had gone further in our knowledge of each other, and of the Sacred Fire, too. While Thomas had been a companion since we'd left the convent, he was far more now. Marie had wondered if it would change anything, being wed; I knew now it changed much, though not yet everything. It felt perhaps like shoring up a sturdy bridge. It would not need to bear more weight, necessarily, but there was comfort in knowing it could, knowing it was that much more secure against dilapidation. And, I'll admit, I was excited to be able to express my love to Thomas in ways we wouldn't previously.

Despite the warmth, there was some grief at leaving Tabitha. The woman from the apothecary came to work for her, so I mourned not that she would need help. But she had become a stalwart friend, perhaps even something like a mother to me. On that road south, I prayed to Our Father to see her again, perhaps if we passed through Holden again someday.

Now I know I would not, and I fear I never will again. Not, at least, on this side of the veil.

Coming Soon!

Don't miss the next installment in the *Spirit Wind* series!

Rae-Anna, Thomas, and Mahmoud reach castle Fosse just as winter arrives, and are welcomed by roaring hearths and a storeroom packed for the long cold nights to come.

Lord and Lady Pendrel seemed pleased to give them shelter, though furtive glances and strained conversation send more than just Rae-Anna's Sacred Fire to flickering.

And soon, between the whispers of the servants and the incessant japes of the gregarious but enigmatic court jester, they learn castle Fosse is haunted by yet another evil—ancient, malignant...and, some might say, mythological.

United in one flesh, Rae-Anna and Thomas are as prepared as they can be for their next supernatural battle in *A Fault to Fear*.

Coming 2024!

Scripture References

Author's note: When the Sacred Fire speaks directly to Rae-Anna, he uses the names of the Trinity from Scripture. When the characters quote the words, they use the names created for the fiction, as those are the names they know them by.

Chapter 2:

"I send you forth as sheep in the midst of wolves." Matt. 10:16

Chapter 3:

"Be not afraid, but speak, and hold not thy peace: for I am with thee, and no man shall set on thee to hurt thee." Acts 18:9-10

"...who through faith quenched the violence of fire..." Heb. 11:33-34

Chapter 6:

"Fret not thyself because of evildoers." Psalm 37:1

"But if we hope for that we see not, then do we with patience wait for it." Rom. 8:25

Chapter 7:

"I preparest a table before thee in the presence of thine enemies." Psalm 23:5

Chapter 9:

"And these words shall be in thine heart: And thou shalt talk of them when thou sittest in thine house, and when thou walkest by the way, and when thou liest down, and when thou risest up." Deut. 6:6-7

"For if these things be in you, and abound, they make you that ye shall neither be barren nor unfruitful...but he that lacketh these things is blind, and cannot see afar off, and hath forgotten that he was purged from his old sins." 2 Peter 1:8-9

"But seek ye first the kingdom of God, and his righteousness..." Matt 6:33

"Henceforth I call you not servants...but I have called you friends." John 15:15

"If we believe not, yet he abideth faithful: he cannot deny himself." 2 Tim. 2:13

"Thou hast turned for me my mourning into dancing: thou hast put off my sackcloth, and girded me with gladness; to the end that my glory may sing praise to thee, and not be silent." Psalm 30:11-12

Chapter 11:

"Now no chastening for the present seemeth to be joyous, but grievous: nevertheless afterward it yieldeth the peaceable fruit of righteousness unto them which are exercised thereby." Heb. 12:11

"Whither is thy beloved gone, O thou fairest among women? whither is thy beloved turned aside? that we may seek him with thee." Song. 6:1

Chapter 12:

"When the wicked, even mine enemies and my foes, came upon me to eat up my flesh, they stumbled and fell. Though an host should encamp against me, my heart shall not fear: though war should rise against me, in this will I be confident." Psalm 27:2-3

"I sleep, but my heart waketh: it is the voice of my beloved that knocketh, saying, Open to me..." Song. 5:2

Chapter 13:

"And walk in love, as Christ also hath loved us, and hath given himself for us an offering and a sacrifice to God for a sweetsmelling savour." Eph. 5:2

"And they overcame him by the blood of the Lamb, and by the word of their testimony; and they loved not their lives unto the death." Rev. 12:11

Chapter 14:

"[the] base things of the world, and things which are despised, hath Our Father chosen..." 1 Cor. 1:28 "...for Our Father seeth not as man seeth; for man looketh on the outward appearance, but Our Father looketh on the heart." 1 Sam. 16:7

"Greater love hath no man than this, that a man lay down his life for his friends." John 15:13

"Let this mind be in you, which was also in The Beloved: he made himself of no reputation, and took upon him the form of a servant." Php. 2:5,7

"whom the Lord loveth he chasteneth..." Heb. 12:6 "...and every branch that beareth fruit, he purgeth it, that it may bring forth more fruit." John 15:2

"But Our Father shall supply all your need according to his riches in glory by The Beloved." Php 4:19.

"we are crucified with The Beloved: nevertheless we live; yet not we, but The Beloved liveth in us: and the life which we now live in the flesh we live by the faith of The Beloved, who loved me, and gave himself for me." Gal 2:20.

"[love] suffereth long, and is kind; envieth not; vaunteth not itself, is not puffed up, doth not behave itself unseemly, seeketh not her own, is not easily provoked, thinketh no evil; rejoiceth not in iniquity, but rejoiceth in the truth; beareth all things, believeth all things, hopeth all things, endureth all things." 1 Cor. 13:4-6

"But he was wounded for our transgressions, he was bruised for our iniquities: the chastisement of our peace was upon him; and with his stripes we are healed." Isa. 53:5

"I bear in my body the marks of Christ." Gal. 6:17

Chapter 16:

"But Our Father hath chosen the foolish things of the world to confound the wise; and Our Father hath chosen the weak things of the world to confound the things which are mighty; and base things of the world, and things which are despised, hath Our Father chosen." 1 Cor. 1:27-28

"Answer not a fool according to his folly." Prov. 26:4

"Therefore shall a man leave his father and his mother, and shall cleave unto his wife: and they shall be one flesh." Gen. 2:24

Acknowledgements

Time again to remember all who made this thing possible:

My Betas and ARC readers, for their eager anticipation of drafts, and critical early opinions.

The Faith Family Writer's Group and their critiques, advice, encouragement, and support.

The coordinators and designers at GetCovers for their thrilling covers.

And, of course, my wife and family for continued support and devotion, and letting me leave the house for a few hours a week to get this done.

About the Author

Daniel Dydek is a multi-genre author with his sweeping epic fantasy series The Triumvirs, and his supernatural suspense series, Spirit Wind, has already garnered two Finalist awards from Realm Makers. Besides writing, he also enjoys a personal relationship with Jesus Christ, mountain biking, reading, coffee shops, book stores, and Durango Colorado. He lives in Canton Ohio with his wife and son and two cats.

Support for the Author

First, thank you for reading this story on whichever medium you chose—Kindle, KU, or paperback. Your support means dreams come true! If you loved the story, there are a lot of ways to continue supporting the author FOR FREE. Here's a few:

1. Subscribe to the newsletter on danieldydek.com

2. Tell your friends!

3. Leave a review on Goodreads, Amazon, Barnes & Noble, or on your social media. (This is probably the greatest support of all, because we love hearing what people enjoyed about the book! Plus, you know, algorithms...)

4. Request your local library to get a copy

All these things help promote the books, and encourage the author to keep writing stories you'll love!

—The Beorn Publishing Team

The Triumvirs epic fantasy series

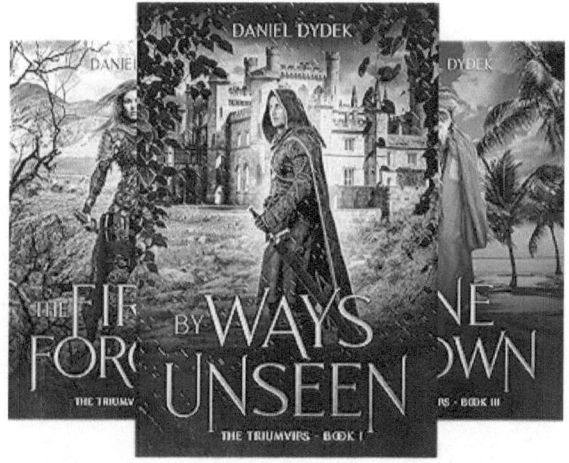

Centuries ago, the world of Oren was ravaged by uncontrolled magic during the Wizards War. In the wake of such devastation and evil, the God of All took three wizards and established for them a Room, of darkness and consciousness, and placed before them a great table whose appearance is of translucent slate, through which they might call up visions of the lands, entering when needed. Few even know these former wizards exist, and their work will always be credited to brave men and women of the world who were faithful in their obedience.

These wizards' task is keeping the peace, of prompting action against the forces of evil. They answer still to the God of All, but retain autonomy. He named them The Triumvirate, and over the centuries twenty-two Triumvirs have guided Oren through wars, famines, pestilences, and the rising and falling of countless empires.

Now, in this current Age of men, will come their most difficult battle.

Amazon search: The Triumvirs Dydek

Spirit Wind Christian suspense series

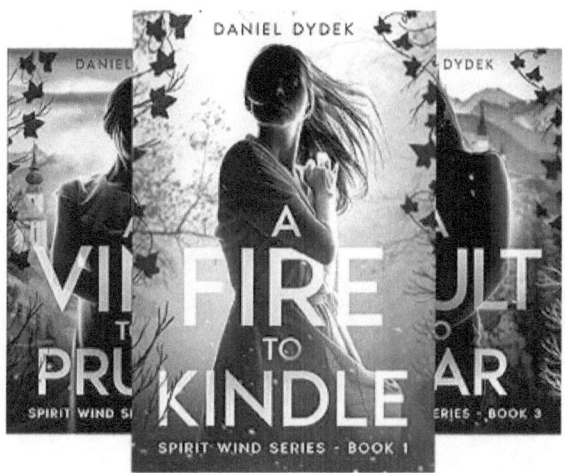

Cursed with left-handedness, then cursed with fire.

Except the fire seems to comfort, to strengthen, to speak wisdom. Wisdom like:

"The wind bloweth where it listeth, and thou hearest the sound thereof, but canst not tell whence it cometh, and whither it goeth: so is every one that is born of the Spirit."

And so Rae-Anna is borne on itinerant winds, never knowing what danger she'll be asked to face. But she knows this: it will always be demonic. And she will never be alone.

Amazon search: Spirit Wind Dydek